HEN FEVER

A SAPPHIC VICTORIAN ROMANCE

OLIVIA WAITE

For Elysabeth Grace, for loaning me Walter
and for Charles, who makes every day a holiday.

"A prudent general will calculate the risks and probabilities of an engagement before he offers battle to the enemy; and so the intended winner of cups, goblets, &c., will scan the capabilities of his establishment before he makes his entries, and sets his hens."
— The Poultry Chronicle, Vol. 3, 1855

1

---

*E**ngland, November 1856*

      The Reverend Lloyd mopped his glistening brow and ascended the pulpit. It wasn't the temperature making him perspire. The air was chilled by the stone walls of the church, and the wintry sunlight filtered cooler still through the glass saints keeping watch over the vicar's shoulder.

The faces of his congregation, however, were ablaze with zeal. Not for the faith, or his sermon—never that, in his memory—but for the great contest they waged every December. The echoes of who achieved glorious victory—and who fell in shameful defeat —would draw up battle lines in the village for the next twelve months.

He couldn't stop the Bickerton Christmas Poultry Show—but perhaps he could prevent its worst excesses from corrupting the souls of his flock.

Just because it had never succeeded before was no reason not to try. It was his duty as a man of God.

Even if it made him feel like Samson after Delilah'd been at him with the shears.

He cleared his throat, braced himself, and began: "Again, I

considered all travail, and every right work, that for this a man is envied of his neighbor. This is also vanity and vexation of spirit."

Please, he wanted to beg them in plainer language. *Please remember that there are more important things than chickens.*

The widowed Mrs. Outerbridge acknowledged the verse with a nod of her head, the dyed plumes on her hat bobbing with the motion. In his pew behind her, lonely Mr. Brome shifted slightly to clear his view, the better to glare at the vicar, who tried not to take it as a personal affront.

Years before, when the Reverend Lloyd was new to St. Gilbert's and still sunny about his prospects and his parish, Mrs. Outerbridge's husband and Mr. Brome's wife had indulged in an affair. This torrid passion had been discovered when Mr. Outerbridge collapsed during a bout of lovemaking, and Mrs. Brome ran a quarter mile in the rain for the doctor. Alas, Mr. Outerbridge was beyond human help, and Mrs. Brome caught a mortal chill and passed a few weeks later.

The surviving spouses turned the full force of shame and grief upon one another, with their main field of combat the Bantam Class rankings at the annual Christmas fair.

In the darkness of his secret heart, where the most unspiritual thoughts were forever creeping from the soil, the vicar had sometimes considered that the wrong spouses had perished. He'd briefly indulged himself in the fantasy of starting his sermon a few verses earlier, with the far more pointed: "Wherefore I praised the dead who are already dead more than the living who are yet alive."

But experience had taught him that there was such a thing as too much honesty, and that Mrs. Outerbridge in particular had a door of iron on her mind that would allow no uninvited thoughts admittance. He could stand at the pulpit and rail against her every failing, precisely and in depth, and it would merely roll off her as she curled up snug in the belief that he was talking about anyone and everyone else.

The vicar continued, trying to make the small church ring with the sound of his voice, tolling out well-polished phrases about the poison of envy and the emptiness of earthly rewards.

But soon the Reverend Lloyd began to realize he'd gravely misjudged his audience. Gazes were sharpening, and spines straightening. The glint of that horrible eagerness was beginning to sparkle in every eye that met his. It was clear that every mention of strife was firing his flock's determination, every warning about envy was whetting their desire to take home the first-place cup.

He could *see* it, in the way each person's glance cut to their favorite rival when they thought he wouldn't notice. There was Miss Rushcliff, all maiden modesty—except where the corners of her lips curled up smugly as she caught the baleful glower of Miss Inch. They'd been fast friends once, until they'd caught the fancy. Now rumor was Miss Inch had trained her Pinwheel Bantams to attack Miss Rushcliff's Scots Dumpies on sight.

There in the last pew, Mr. Finglass of the Cock and Apple was working his hands, undoubtedly cracking his knuckles. With every crack—not that the vicar could hear them, thank heavens, but he knew the sound far too well—Mr. and Mrs. Campbell-Cole's sinews went a little stiffer across the aisle. Lucky Mr. Finglass only had ten fingers, or the couple might have done him violence.

A disagreement about the results of the Brahma judging some years back had never been resolved. The Campbell-Coles' haberdashery shop stood across the way from the tavern, and Mr. Finglass more than once had been heard to suggest their hats as receptacles for anyone who'd overindulged in the Cock and Apple's strongest ale.

And then there was the spinster.

Miss Lydia Wraxhall had just turned thirty when the Reverend Lloyd arrived at St. Gilbert's. She was mid-forties now, with silver streaks in her dark hair—but her brown eyes still glowed, and her frequent smile turned an otherwise plain face into something striking and attractive. She was a soft, kind, thoughtful,

3

comforting sort of woman, and at first it had quite baffled the vicar that none of the village's available men had taken the trouble to court her.

There had been one or two proposals the lady had turned down, he understood now. And what's more, he understood why there had never been more: Miss Wraxhall was, to put it simply, too good.

She radiated affability more than anyone he'd ever met. You liked it at first—until it started to feel like standing in sunlight for days on end, when all you wanted was darkness and a good night's rest. That secret, horrible part of the vicar's soul had whispered some very uncharitable thoughts about nobody liking to feel like they were the worst person in any conversation.

And it wasn't just that air of hers which infuriated. Whereas everyone else in the poultry show had a particular rival and a particular favorite breed, Miss Wraxhall chose a different kind of bird every year, hopping from class to class and threatening everyone else's equilibrium. Because of course she was good at showing birds, too: her chickens' plumage always shone, their points were inevitably impeccable and received high marks from the judges who came down by train from larger, busier Birmingham. And every triumph only made the others all the more determined to best her next time.

The Reverend Lloyd didn't think she was doing it deliberately, but the fact remained that Miss Wraxhall alone stirred up more venom around the poultry show than any other single participant.

Even now she was watching him, hands folded serenely, eyes fixed on his face. Listening as attentively as if St. Gilbert himself had stepped out of the stained glass and addressed the congregation. The vicar flushed as he noticed a few infelicities of phrasing that had somehow escaped his notice until this moment.

He'd wanted to bring this sermon to a thunderous, powerful end; instead, he stammered and stumbled his way through the final paragraph, and could feel nothing but nauseous relief to hear his flock begin the familiar words of the Creed. *He will come again in glory to judge the living and the dead…*

Not for the first time, the Reverend Lloyd had the unsettling thought that his parishioners spent most of the year courting judgment, when they would do better cultivating grace or mercy instead. He hoped they never had cause to truly regret it.

Amen, his congregation said.

~ ~ ~ ~

The Cochin and red hens were still snug in their roosts, and the old Pinwheel Bantam hen (Best of Breed, said the shining cup on Lydia's bedroom shelf) was happily scratching away beneath the apple tree—but she was alone. The Snortington's Red cockerel that usually stuck close by her side was nowhere to be seen. A light dusting of snow had fallen in the night, so it only took moments for Lydia to find the tracks that led to a spot in the fence where the wire mesh had been tugged loose from the wooden beam.

Walter had escaped.

Lydia sighed, and first of all repaired the break. She'd thought Walter too daft to manage this kind of trouble. The more fool her. Snortington's Reds were docile breeds, determined homebodies who usually stayed close to other fowl or their chosen people. A snuggling chicken, she would have said, and sweet-tempered Walter had never shown the slightest inclination to wander before today.

She didn't have time for this, not really. She was supposed to help her mother pack a basket for Mrs. Kaur's charity bazaar, and then she had to stop in to see Mr. Beconshaw and Mr. Finglass with a few things from her father. Dr. Wraxhall may have retired from his medical practice, but he still kept up care for a few of his long-standing patients. Chasing after a stray bird was not where a daughter's first duty lay.

Wayward chickens, wayward children.

5

She and Peter had both been disappointments to their parents. It had been a secret shame they carried between them. They'd tried to make up for it in every way they could: Lydia at home, and Peter in the army. Now Peter was gone, and Lydia was feeling the strain of trying to be two perfect children at once.

Except... it was winter. Despite the inconvenience that might vex them, her mother and father were in no danger if she changed her plans for the day. Whereas Walter, edible and sheltered and a little stupid, could find any number of ways to get hurt. There were eagles in the world, and dogs, and hungry people who couldn't afford to pass up a fresh bit of poultry, if it came blithely strolling toward them in the lane.

Walter needed her more.

She finished her repair, gathered a pocketful of scratch grains, and set off to find the little ingrate.

Not ten steps out of the yard, Walter's footprints intercepted a confusing muddle of snow and muck and sodden leaves. A few steps past that, the tracks of several birds led off into the forest. Walter's were slightly larger than the others, and easy to spot—but there were at least five, maybe six other fowl that had passed this way. All at once, too, from the way the tracks were layered.

Lydia pulled her scarf close about her neck and ventured into the greenwood.

Tall trees cast the path in deep shadow, and dry needles muffled the thump of Lydia's winter boots. The trail at least was clear enough. Two of the smaller birds had kept to the outside, while Walter's tracks zigged back and forth along the centerline. Almost as though—Lydia paused and frowned, as a chill skittered down the back of her neck—as though he were being herded. But no lost feathers littered the trail, no droplets of blood or torn-up earth to mark a skirmish.

Lydia climbed higher, as the prints led up the wooded hill and toward the ruins.

Bickerton Abbey wore the memories of its long-dead splendor like a tattered cloak over ancient bones. The forest hadn't quite crept up the hill and reclaimed the stone arches and fluted columns, but it was sending out grasping fingers in the form of brambles and moss and grasses. The snow had whitened stone and growth alike, and the undisturbed banks glowed like marble in the shafts of sunlight pouring through the empty windowpanes. As Lydia strode through the tumbled walls of the nave—ducking her head in reverence, since after all this had once been holy ground—she could hear the unmistakeable soft sounds of happy chickens echoing from somewhere amid the columns.

She stepped around the northernmost column and stopped, shocked.

One column had fallen in a slant against the wall, making a bit of shelter against the world. Beneath it Walter's red plumes were unmistakeable, vivid as flame against all that old stone.

He was the bright, beating heart of a little huddle of feathered bodies.

Six—yes, she'd been right—little grey bundles were cozied up on every side of him, on a nest of grass and branches. Six grey hens, bantam-sized—but as they moved, flashes of silver caught her eye and made her gasp aloud.

They were Bickerton Greys.

She hadn't set eyes on that particular plumage in a good ten years, but it wasn't the kind of thing a chicken fancier forgot. Bright silver lacing shimmering over a softer dove grey. The Bickerton Grey was a local breed, spun off of the more popular Sebright by some scientific-minded farmer in the early half of the century. All of them, every last bird, had been lost years ago. A few people had claimed occasional sightings in the deepest part of the woods—but they were clever birds, quick and canny and fierce. Nobody had ever found a nest of theirs.

Until now.

Among the hens, Walter tilted his head, chucking affably as though trying to introduce his old friend to his new paramours. The Greys shifted warily, more alert to the threat Lydia represented.

She tugged off her mitten, put her hand in her pocket, and scattered the ground in front of her with scratch.

Walter made for it at once—but one of the Greys objected, squawking a warning and shoving her smaller shape in between Walter and the scratch.

Lydia took a step back as a show of good faith, making soft and soothing sounds.

The Greys were not fooled. They packed themselves in closer, muttering what sounded like chicken curses and ruffling their feathers in pique.

Walter looked at Lydia and clucked an apology: *Buk.*

Lydia pulled her mitten back on and considered the situation. It looked like this feral flock was staking a claim to her prize cockerel.

Well, he wasn't a prize cockerel yet—but Lydia knew her birds, and Walter was the best Snortington's Red she'd ever seen. From the tip of his rose comb to the gorgeous fall of his crimson tail, his points were impeccable. His temperament was just as winning, as he was easy to handle and adored being brushed and buffed to a gleaming shine. Lydia had planned for him to dazzle the judges of the Black-Breasted and Other Reds Class.

And he still could. Two months yet before the show. Plenty of time for her to coax Walter back to his home yard—and for her to capitalize on this new opportunity.

Silver feathers flashed in the sun, but not nearly so bright as the future now unfolding in Lydia's imagination.

It wasn't every day you got to resurrect an entire breed.

Bickerton Greys were small, and didn't carry as much meat on their breast as larger fowl did—but they were tender and notoriously tasty, and what was more, they were some of the strongest winter layers anyone in the village had ever raised. Their eggs had a soft green hue—inherited from the Araucanas in their lineage—and they laid on average one a day from October until March, when fresh eggs sold at much higher premiums than the rest of the year.

It was one thing to raise a single prize bird. Lydia had done that several years running: you hatched your chicks carefully and selected the best and presented them well, and the judges took care of the rest.

But a whole new breed—a rare and glorious bird that had been thought lost for a decade... That was the way to make a mark on the world.

Lydia had thought her time for making a mark had long passed. But perhaps she had been guilty of impatience. Perhaps Fate had only been slow, rather than indifferent.

A sudden shadow fell across the snow. Walter cried out, the same shriek he used when he spotted a hawk or an owl sweeping overhead.

Lydia whirled, heart in her throat.

A woman on horseback, silhouetted in the Gothic arch that opened to the north. Sunlight flickered and shifted behind her as she dismounted, turning her silhouette into something strange and monstrous that made the breath catch in Lydia's throat.

Crop in hand, the woman strode forward into the ruined church.

Lydia pressed hard against the column at her back and felt the cool stone scrape against the wool of her coat.

Once the woman was inside, the shift in light let Lydia make out the new arrival in more detail. A heavy woolen skirt with flannel petticoats, all short enough to show the worn boots beneath. A sturdy coat so green it was nearly black, with black straps across the breast in the military style. A small hat over chestnut hair liberally peppered with white, and a thick muffler wrapped for warmth around the lower half of her face. She put up one black-gloved hand and pulled down the muffler, revealing a mouth that was one long sensual berry-colored curve.

But above that mouth her eyes were grey and furious and they sliced through Lydia like a saber. "You're trespassing, madam," she said.

"Oh!" Shame at even the hint of illegality spurred Lydia

forward, hand extended. "You're right—I'm terribly sorry. My name is Lydia Wraxhall, and I'm only here to retrieve my lost rooster."

The woman shook her hand, the leather of her glove slippery beneath Lydia's worsted mitten, and said nothing.

Lydia pressed for more. "You must be one of the new tenants at Thornycroft Hall."

"Mrs. Harriet Boyne," the woman said. "And we aren't tenants. The Hall belongs to us."

"Really?" Lydia leaned forward. "Everyone assumed you had rented it from Lady Eccleston's heir."

The woman raised her chin. "We are Lady Eccleston's heirs."

Really? Lydia almost asked again, but bit her tongue.

The whole village knew there was a cousin somewhere in the family, and they'd assumed he would inherit when word had come about Lady Eccleston's death. Speculation had been fierce: the house had stood empty for months and months, boarded up when the lady took a wild hare and turned volunteer nurse in the early days of the war. Her solicitors were in London, not likely to linger on Bickerton Green for a gossip, or to drop hints about the estate over pints at the Cock and Apple.

But for Lady Eccleston to leave Thornycroft to this stranger? Or group of strangers, more precisely—she'd said *we*. There were five new inhabitants, according to Mrs. Jeremy, who did for Mr. Finglass three days a week and whose niece had just been hired as a kitchen maid at the Hall. Mr. Finglass had been concerned they might be paying better wages than he was, and that it would give Mrs. Jeremy ideas.

Privately Lydia hoped it did: Mr. Finglass was gruff and careless, and Mrs. Jeremy doubtless deserved a higher wage. Fanny had tried to clean for him once before coming to Lydia's, and she'd barely lasted a week.

Lydia shook herself. She was wasting time in petty speculation, when there were interesting problems to solve. She nodded a head at the flock. "Are these hens yours?"

"No," Mrs. Boyne said, a denial like the shutting of a door. "They're wild birds."

Lydia's hopes bounced up again. "So you wouldn't mind if I took them off your hands?"

"Of course you can't. They're on my land."

Lydia smothered a groan of dismay beneath a perfectly polite smile. "Are you breeding them?"

A flicker of cold amusement in those steel-grey eyes. "Rather the reverse—we've been eating them."

Lydia gasped aloud. *Eating them!*

Mrs. Boyne tilted her head, as if observing the results of an experiment, and said: "They're quite delicious."

A whole flock of Bickerton Greys, and this woman had been serving them up as meals? It hardly mattered that their flavor was part of why they'd been bred in the first place. It was an appalling waste.

Lydia swiftly found her voice again. "Do you know what kind of birds these are, Mrs. Boyne?"

"No," the woman said, all amusement gone from those grey eyes. She looked as cold as winter itself in her dark coat.

"They're all that's left of a unique village breed," Lydia went on. Surely once she explained, the woman would see reason. "Every ten years or so, a wild storm comes through the village; the last one knocked down every chicken coop in town. Most birds were recovered over the next few days—and everyone now builds their coops like fortresses, to prevent another such disaster —but the Bickerton Greys were better at eluding capture than most other fowl. They escaped into the woods, every last one of them. Most people believe they've died out." She waved at the hens, who were flanking Walter as though ready to follow their general into battle. "These six may be all that are left. I raise chickens, you see, not for meat but to show—and I'm begging you, let me take these and try and restore the lineage. I'll compensate you in any way you think fair." She stopped, and swallowed hard.

11

Mrs. Boyne did not appear to be listening. She was staring with narrowed eyes at the Bickerton Greys, who were staring back with equal suspicion. One of the hens even had a head cocked at the same angle; Lydia bit her lip to stifle a poorly timed anxious giggle.

"I assume you know easier ways of catching live chickens than simply chasing them?" Mrs. Boyne said at last. "Or more dignified ways, at least."

Lydia nearly collapsed with relief. "I do," she said. "The best way is to wait until dark, when they're sleeping. You use a covered lantern, with just enough light to make out the shape of the bird, and you simply pick them up, holding their wings tight to the body." She mimed the gesture, mittens held about a chicken-width apart.

Mrs. Boyne's wintry expression froze further. "You cannot be serious."

Lydia smiled sunnily. "You could always try running after them. In broad daylight. Where everyone can see."

Mrs. Boyne frowned and took one step toward the hens.

Instantly the Greys started a clamor, clucking over one another and ruffling feathers to seem as large as possible. Walter, in the middle of so much anger, caught some of the hens' fear and began echoing their alarm.

Mrs. Boyne stepped back again, and the Greys subsided into a mutter.

Lydia could feel smug words curling on the tip of her tongue, and bit down hard to keep them back.

At last the other woman sighed. "If you come back tonight to help us capture the hens, I'll send you home with half the flock. In addition to your lost rooster, of course."

"Of course," Lydia said. "With your permission, I'll just wait here until then."

Mrs. Boyne blinked at her several times. "Until nightfall? Alone?"

"I'm not going to leave Walter on his own out here," Lydia

said. "He's never been out of the yard before. He doesn't know how to protect himself."

Mrs. Boyne looked from Walter, in a cozy nest surrounded by defenders, to Lydia, standing on bare snow and rock. "If you're sure," she said doubtfully.

"The sky looks clear, there's no wind to speak of, and I have some bread and cheese with me and a book in my coat pocket," Lydia replied. "I've had worse days than this, I assure you."

Something haunted passed over Mrs. Boyne's face, so stark that Lydia herself felt the chill of it even through all her layers of wool and warmth. "Suit yourself, Mrs. Wraxhall."

"It's Miss," Lydia returned, and that berry-hued mouth quirked acknowledgement as Mrs. Boyne turned away. With easy grace she passed back through the arch, mounted her horse, and vanished over the snowy fields and fences beyond.

Somehow, though Mrs. Boyne's grey gaze had been cold the entire time, the world felt a little icier with her gone. Lydia turned her coat collar up against the back of her neck, and settled in for a long day's wait.

---

2

*H*arriet rode down one hill and around another and there was Thornycroft Hall, smoking from every chimney in defiance of the cold. She took Patience to the stable and gave her the rubdown the mare deserved, then ducked in through the kitchen because that was the quickest way of getting warm.

Fires crackled, stovetops hissed, and great iron ovens poured out heat as the kitchen maids and the undercook worked. The sounds of soap and water echoed softly from the scullery, as a third maid washed the last of the breakfast things. Harriet stripped off her gloves and hat and breathed in the smell of roasting meat and baking bread, hot enough to almost singe the back of her throat.

It still didn't touch the little ball of ice where her heart used to be, but it helped some.

At a long scarred table to the side, Lizzie Crangle was poring over her cookbooks, planning the Hall's future meals. At other homes this would have been the duty of the sole mistress of the house: here there were more than enough mistresses to go around: Mrs. Goodfellow had the blue parlor for all her sewing supplies, Mr. Dixit the library for his charity work, Mrs. Marwood her sitting room, and Harriet the grounds and gardens. All their little habits, relics of the war, like scars over unseen wounds.

Mrs. Crangle's domain was the kitchens, because she now refused to let anyone go hungry. She raised her head, all ruddy cheeks and soft eyes. "Sauce is about to burn, Mary," she called out, and the undercook hurried to remove a pan from the heat.

"Morning, Crangle," Harriet said.

"Morning, Boyne," the cook replied, with a flash of a grin.

Harriet snagged a slice of toast and cheese from the hearth, where Mrs. Crangle always kept something warm in case someone wandered by in need of feeding. "How would you feel about keeping chickens?" Harriet asked.

Crangle lifted a brow. "For eggs or for meat?"

"Eggs first, meat later, I should think."

The cook considered this as she reached onto the shelf behind her and snagged a jar of honey, with which she anointed Harriet's toast and cheese. "There's a small run off the kitchen garden. I believe Lady Eccleston had all the birds sold off before she took ship—but the coop's there. Be more convenient if we had eggs of our own, that's certain." That grin flashed again, the bright one that Harriet was seeing more and more often since they'd moved into the Hall. "Don't tell me you're getting tired of bringing back wild birds already."

"Hardly." Harriet took another bite of toast, and closed her eyes to luxuriate in the mingled sweetness and savor. She swallowed with a sigh. "Turns out our wild birds perhaps aren't so wild after all—and someone has offered to help us catch and keep the lot of them."

"Someone has, eh?" Lizzie Crangle's eyes widened with curiosity. "Who might that be?"

Wraxhall, Harriet thought, but didn't say. She wanted to confirm her suspicions first. Memory was a flighty, disreputable thing where the war was concerned. "One of the neighbors I met near the ruins. Her rooster had wandered in there, lured by our wild hens."

"It's a desperate woman who has to come all the way here in search of a cock."

Harriet choked on a mouthful of sticky, cheesy crumbs.

Mary called out for the kitchen maids to help her roll out dough for meat pies. Still snickering, Crangle rose to supervise the pie-making, and Harriet swallowed the last of her food and hurried upstairs to the library.

Calling it a library was giving it more credit than it deserved. The room was more properly a study, with only two sets of bookshelves built into the high walls on either side of the window. Arun Dixit had already filled all those to bursting, however, and had ordered more shelves from a local carpenter to be installed along the remaining walls.

At present the journalist was sitting at his desk, the side of which had been set flush against the window-frame so Mr. Dixit could have as wide a view as possible of the land and wood and hills that Thornycroft faced. His dark hair had grown long on the voyage home, and the thick curls bounced insistently as he worked.

As Harriet entered, he signed with a flourish the letter he was writing, and set it on top of a similar stack. A new piece of paper was immediately placed on the blotter, pale and stark where his brown hand pressed sensitive fingertips against it.

Harriet planted herself by the warmth of the fireplace and coughed gently. "Mr. Dixit, I wondered if I could ask you to look up something from your notes?"

His pen stopped, and he blinked up at her.

Harriet repeated her request, to make sure he'd heard all of it.

The journalist nodded and reached for the notebook he always carried in his breast pocket. "What is it you need, Mrs. Boyne?"

"I was trying to recall the surname of Lady Eccleston's soldier. The one who—"

"Yes," Mr. Dixit murmured. "The one who." His long fingers fluttered the pages until they found the one they sought.

"Wraxhall," he said. "Peter Wraxhall—later Sergeant Wraxhall. Battlefield promotion after Inkerman."

"Thank you," Harriet said. "That was all."

Mr. Dixit nodded and returned to his letters. He sent them daily to various papers: to the *Times*, the *Midlands County Herald*, the *Birmingham Daily Post*. Not to mention all the individual correspondence to wives, widows, clergy, regimental commanders, local magistrates, and philanthropists. He may not have been sending reportage to a newspaper any longer, but he still spent nearly every waking hour writing something—and still about the war, even as it was winding down.

All in all, it was good that Lady Eccleston had left them her fortune as well as her house. There was no question of Mr. Dixit being able to afford paper, postage, and ink.

Harriet took her time walking back down the long staircase. So —the name Wraxhall had been familiar for a reason. Mr. Dixit's notes had brought his face back up out of the depths of oblivion: a broad smile and crinkles at the corner of his eyes, sturdy hands, skin weathered by long years on campaign. And more than that, the sense of sunlight, of a heart so warm he made you feel like summer even in the middle of the coldest winter you'd ever known.

And then later: the flush of fever, the restlessness, the exhaustion and final fatigue.

Harriet shook off that last part of the memory. It wasn't how the man would have wanted to be remembered. It certainly wasn't the kind of thing that would comfort anyone grieving his loss.

At least the woman in the ruins was his sister, not his wife or mother. *It's Miss*, she'd said—even as she'd stated her intention to stay out, all day, in the cold, with a coat barely worth the name and only a bit of bread and cheese to eat the whole while.

At this point Harriet realized she'd been pacing the entrance hall, walking restlessly back and forth over the stones between the sitting-room door and the lowest stair. She made her feet stop.

17

They stopped.

Her hands had only just gotten properly warm again after the ride. The parlor fire was lit and merry, crackling in the hearth. Mr. Dixit had bedecked the mantel with evergreen boughs only yesterday, and set twists of silver paper in the branches to catch the firelight and gleam like caught stars. One of Mrs. Goodfellow's quilts was draped invitingly across the back of the sofa—one of the floral ones, not one of her unsettling ones with fires or battlefields made out of the tattered scraps of dead men's clothes—and Harriet knew it would feel marvelous wrapped around her shoulders. Mrs. Crangle would be happy to send up more bread and cheese, or some cake from the pantry, and a pot of good tea.

But no matter how warm Harriet got or how much coziness she tried to surround herself with, that ball of ice in her breast wasn't going anywhere. It was her own little souvenir of the Crimea; a stubborn, frozen chunk of the war that not even the hottest fire seemed to touch. The relentless chill of it was a spur, sending her outdoors to walk or ride or run until exhaustion forced her to turn back.

Might as well do something useful with it.

Her mind made up, she released the hold on herself. Her feet were glad to be moving as she headed back down to the kitchen, where Mrs. Crangle positively lit up when Harriet explained what she wanted.

Patience was feeding and in need of a rest, so Harriet saddled her sister Folly instead. The mare was clearly itching for a run, so Harriet made doubly sure everything was firmly fixed before climbing into the saddle and letting the mare have her head. Folly's hooves flew over the turf, kicking up the light snow until it glittered in the sunlight; Harriet indulged and took her the long way toward the ruins, around the base of the two hills and then up to approach the old church from the west rather than the north. She tied Folly securely and took down the basket, then made her way into the abbey.

Enough time had passed by now that the light had changed. Miss Wraxhall had seated herself against the base of a column, knees high, black coat and skirts all tucked close around her. Despite her mourning clothes she seemed to have collected all the sunlight around herself: the silver in her hair flashed almost white with it, and the pages of her book were bright enough to blind.

The ground in front of her was scattered with seed. The tall red rooster—Walter, Harriet recalled—had found his courage and was happily pecking at the grains. A few of the grey hens had joined him, though Harriet noticed they stayed carefully out of Miss Wraxhall's reach. The rest of the hens were keeping watch, and called a warning when Harriet took another step forward.

The grey hens nudged Walter back to the safety of the nest.

Miss Wraxhall looked up, blinking in bafflement, as though slowly freeing herself from a spell. "Mrs. Boyne?" she said.

Harriet felt briefly ridiculous. The basket weighed heavy in her hands, and Miss Wraxhall was looking at her as though she were some sort of apparition. Nothing for it but to proceed, and hope the feeling passed swiftly. "Bread and cheese didn't sound all that filling," she said, "so I had Mrs. Crangle make us up a picnic basket."

She set the basket down on the path and began to unpack its contents.

A small blanket to spread as protection from the cold, icy ground. Pork sandwiches, boiled beef, and a flask of tea still warm enough to scald. A bottle of cider, apple tarts, and a loaf of fresh bread with several of Mrs. Crangle's best jellies. More cheeses, cold chicken, and two of the delectable pigeon pies Mrs. Crangle had made yesterday.

Miss Wraxhall's eyes got wider with every item Harriet unpacked. She gave a little laugh. "Don't you think Mrs. Crangle may have overdone things a bit?"

"Better too much than too little."

"I suppose so—but goodness, I hope you're planning to help me with all of this!"

Harriet eyed the pigeon pie and knew herself for a weak woman. "If you're sure," she said.

Miss Wraxhall went for the sandwiches, while Harriet poured them both tea in handleless cups. The pigeon pie was even better than yesterday, so Harriet ate it slowly and deliberately set the other one in front of Miss Wraxhall, away from temptation.

Miss Wraxhall took the hint, took a bite of pigeon pie, and let out a sound of such animal satisfaction that Harriet felt herself blush to have heard it. The woman's eyes closed, lashes dark against her cheek, and the tip of her tongue licked out to get every bit of flavor from her lips.

Suddenly temptation had quite another object.

Miss Wraxhall's eyes opened—brown, Harriet noticed now. Warm, chocolate brown so velvet-rich you could happily drown in it. "Do you think Mrs. Crangle would give me this recipe?"

"I'm certain she would," Harriet said. "Though you might have to bribe her into it."

Miss Wraxhall smiled, eyes warming with mischief. "And what kind of bribe works best on Mrs. Crangle?"

"Other recipes," Harriet said. "Good wine, or brandy, or whiskey. Preserves or pickles, if you make them. Things that last. Things that can be saved against future need." She shifted a little. "Of course, she might give you the recipe free and clear just to thank you for helping with the hens. She's excited to have a source of eggs closer to home than the Bickerton market."

Miss Wraxhall chuckled, sounding very like one of those hens herself. "We haven't gotten them home yet—I'll wait to ask about the pie until the flock is safe at Thornycroft."

"You seem to have coaxed them into less suspicion, at least. It's more than I would be able to do in one morning." Harriet cast a skeptical eye at the hens semi-bristling in their nest. As if they knew their kind was being feasted upon not a dozen steps away. "You might have lured them all the way home before much longer."

Miss Wraxhall sat straight up. "I do not steal chickens!"

Delivered in the same tone of voice in which one might say *I do not devour babies!*

"I didn't say stealing—I said luring."

Miss Wraxhall frowned. "Is there a difference?"

"Luring implies that you gave the chickens a choice."

Miss Wraxhall laughed, still uneasy, but clearly trying not to be. "First bribery, and now theft—sorry, *luring,*" she said. "Where did you come by so many vices, Mrs. Boyne?"

"In the army, Miss Wraxhall."

That soft gaze sharpened. "Your husband was a soldier?"

Harriet nodded.

"My brother was a soldier."

Harriet nodded again. "In the 19th."

Miss Wraxhall's eye had an edge now. "You knew him?"

What could Harriet possibly say to that? After Harriet was widowed, in the worst month of her life, a stranger—her brother —had saved her and her friends. He'd been honest, brave, and kind, even when everything around them was mud and blood and disaster. He'd cheered them all with an ease that still left Harriet breathless—then he'd died uselessly in anguish from an ugly disease, and been buried in a sullen little plot of land on the other side of the world.

The best man she'd ever met had described his sister—this sister—as the best woman he'd ever known. What could you even say to a person like that, about such an irreplaceable loss?

"I knew him," Harriet could only reply.

Miss Wraxhall waited a moment, then seemed to realize Harriet was not going to elaborate. "Did you meet him through Lady Eccleston?"

"No—my husband was in the 19th. He was killed at Alma." While Harriet had been on a ship moored miles away. The ball of ice in her chest was rising now, rolling, climbing into her throat and choking off her words. "I met Lady Eccleston in Scutari."

"At the hospital."

Harriet nodded. That had been—after. After John's death, after

Marwood's, after Peter's. When the army had decreed the widows must go home, and sent their little group back to Scutari with the wounded. Harriet had a letter of introduction, written by Peter to Lady Eccleston, who was a volunteer nurse there—she'd helped them find lodging, and food. And then that lady had fallen sick herself, and died despite all Harriet and her friends' desperate care. Mr. Dixit had drawn up her will in that final fever, and had it witnessed by two of the officers.

And they'd all shipped back to England. Where the survivors had found a fortune and a manor and a world that was so unchanged by war that they could not recognize their place in it. It was a dream, a fairy story they were walking through but never really a part of.

Except every now and then—when the rains blurred out the woods or when the snow fell thick and cold and made everything a sea of empty white. Like now. Then in Harriet's heart everything became low plains, flattened by too many marching feet and iced by the world's indifference. As though the nightmare landscape of war had followed her home and imposed itself on the growing green of England.

She took a sip of tea, desperate for the heat. Her throat creaked with it. "Your brother was a good soldier," she said to Miss Wraxhall. "But more than that: he was a good man. You should be proud of him."

"I am." The reply came so swiftly Harriet blinked at little. Miss Wraxhall was almost glaring at her, fierce as one of her little hens. "I am very proud of my brother," she said again. Almost angrily.

Almost as if…

Harriet's interest prickled. Peter had been the very picture of ideal young English manhood: handsome, energetic, and virtuous —except for one thing.

He'd loved Captain Marwood. Deeply, passionately, and— important when you sprang from English soil—outside what the laws permitted.

And Harriet had the sudden strong impression that Miss Wraxhall knew it.

Something about the defensiveness, the defiance. Harriet had heard it so many times, from so many people. From her own lips, before she'd gone to the Crimea and the kind of laws that felt so all-important at home ceased to have any real meaning.

In war, the only law was power. And power knew no civilians —you were either a combatant or a victim.

Harriet had seen people do terrible things. Theft, rape, all manner of abuses. Two men falling in love didn't even make the list of things she cared to condemn.

"I did not know your brother long," she said again. Hoping the repetition would get the message through in code, if not in concrete words. And then she remembered something. "But I know one thing you don't: Peter Wraxhall did steal chickens."

~ ~ ~ ~

Mrs. Boyne was a puzzle.

She'd barely introduced herself before accusing Lydia of trespassing and insisting on her rights to the long-lost Bickerton Greys. She'd vanished and then reappeared bearing more food than Lydia could eat in a week, like a confused Valkyrie who'd tired of carrying off the souls of the slain and wanted to bring Valhalla's feast down to earth instead. She'd shocked Lydia by mentioning Peter, and her face whenever she talked about the Crimea had sent shivers down Lydia's spine.

And then, out of nowhere, she had smiled.

That berry mouth had curved, and widened, going from a sharp line in a sharp face to something lush and sly and knowing. If all the snow in the Abbey ruins had melted, Lydia wouldn't have been surprised. She was still melting a little herself.

And now she was saying Peter was a thief.

"This was just after Alma," Mrs. Boyne was saying, an echo of that smile lingering on her lips. "Mrs. Marwood and I were still on board the *Shooting Star* as the army moved south toward Sebastopol. Your Peter, my husband John, and Captain Marwood were with them—the captain had been wounded in the arm, and Peter got it in his head nothing would do but a bowl of chicken soup to speed his recovery. Every farmhouse and cottage for miles around had been stripped clean of foodstuffs by the Russian soldiers—and anything they hadn't found our men quickly seized. But the city road was also lined with summer villas that belonged to the wealthy lords and ladies of Sebastopol. Our men fell on these like hard-won prizes, carrying off bedding and furnishings and anything small and shiny. They'd have taken the pianos and chandeliers too, if they'd had a way to carry them."

She cut a glance Lydia's way, so Lydia offered an encouraging nod.

"While everyone else was busy in the house, Peter ducked into the gardens at the back. Somehow the kitchen garden had escaped notice—he found carrots and leeks and then, miraculously, a coop. When they camped that night, they were able to cook up enough soup to feed a dozen of the wounded." She smiled at Lydia again, her grey eyes glittering like chips of ice. "So you see, your brother did steal chickens—but only for the greater good."

Lydia managed a light chuckle, as Mrs. Boyne clearly intended her to be amused. But the thought of Peter, or anyone, having to scrounge for food after a battle was a knife to the heart.

And here she sat with a feast spread out on every side. They had barely made a dent in the picnic basket's contents—the jellies and cheeses hadn't even been touched. Guilt speared through Lydia. "We should take the rest of this to Mrs. Kaur. She's organizing a charity bazaar for the local Patriotic Fund—I'm sure she could find some use for it."

"I believe Mrs. Crangle has already sent several baskets over," Mrs. Boyne replied, but began packing up the remains of their meal all the same. Her smile had vanished, "Until nightfall, Miss Wraxhall." With a nod of her chestnut head, she returned to her horse, leapt into the saddle, and was off again down the hill.

Lydia watched until the snowy landscape swallowed her graceful figure. Shadows shifted, and the sunlight turned thick as the day waned.

Lydia felt something in her fading with it. She'd known Peter had suffered hardship; he'd written her about it often enough. They were not in the habit of hiding things from one another. She'd known, too, about him and Captain Marwood. She'd approved, for whatever such approval was worth. The captain sounded like he made Peter happy more often than not.

The stolen chickens, though... It was one thing to read war stories in print, at a distance. Quite another to hear them from someone who'd lived through them. There was the frightening chance to ask all manner of probing, too-intimate questions: *Were you afraid? Do you feel changed by what you've seen? Are you still grieving?*

Did he suffer terribly at the end?

Worse still: the possibility that you might get an answer.

It forced Lydia face to face with the humbling fact that, deep down, part of her did not want to know.

She didn't want to know such horrible things had happened, especially to people she loved when she could do nothing to save them or soothe their passing. She didn't want to know about strangers in pain, or young soldiers falling, or diseases that brooked no cure.

It was the unworthiest impulse of a common and cowardly soul.

Was this all goodness was? To live in polite ignorance while others fought and died? Walking the same roads every day, on the same errands, never changing, until her proper little steps wore grooves in the cobbles and the hall of her father's house. Until she took her last breath beneath the same roof where she'd breathed her first, and went to sleep in the earth mere steps away. Unloved, unremarked, and unremembered.

Peter had not even been gone a year, and already Lydia feared she had become someone he would not recognize.

A nudge on her elbow. She raised it, and there was Walter, making soft sounds of worry and climbing into her lap. She sighed. A snuggling chicken indeed. She stroked the plumage on his neck, soothing him, and also herself.

The Greys were watching. But this watching had a different quality. There was a kind of anticipation in it now, as if they had reached a détente and now were wondering: *What next?*

Suddenly Lydia was sick to death of goodness.

She was sick of the polite thing, the proper thing, the dutiful thing. She knew now why Peter had joined the army in the first place all those years ago—it got him out, and away from this feeling of suffocation. He'd been older, and braver, and a little wiser than his sister.

She didn't have that option: nobody wanted women in the army. So failing that, what would her soldier brother do, right here, right now?

One of the Bickerton Greys took a step toward her—then another. Testing her. Curious, rather than afraid.

Mrs. Boyne's words rang in her mind like bells: *Luring implies that you gave the chickens a choice.*

Recklessly, Lydia decided that sounded like fine advice.

She braced Walter in her arms and stood. The hens rose as a flock and drifted over, wary but willing, as the rooster in her arms clucked encouragement. Slowly, with Lydia in the lead, they moved down the ruined nave of the church, then down the hill, then into the wood.

The Greys chose every step of the way home.

~ ~ ~ ~

Harriet had barely glanced around Bickerton proper when they moved into the Hall. Now she observed it was a close little place, the church and the green and the tavern all packed tight as if huddled suspiciously against outsiders. The almost-but-not-quite-rude sign of the Cock and Apple was hung with icicles on this frosty morning, as Harriet Boyne marched past on the way to Dr. Wraxhall's house to shout at his thieving daughter.

Oh, she ought to have known that story about catching chickens at night was a joke. She'd let herself get taken in by mourning colors and a pair of soft brown eyes. Never again. God, the way Lizzie Crangle had laughed when she and Arun and Harriet had showed up at the Abbey after sunset, with covered lanterns and a wheelbarrow with a makeshift coop of wood and wire. They'd crept so carefully up the hill—trying not to spook the sleeping birds.

Birds who were, by then, at least a mile away and safely tucked in with Miss Wraxhall's rooster.

Harriet's friends were never going to let her forget it.

Dr. Wraxhall's home had a new gate, but the stone was old, and a century's worth of ivy held the snow close to the walls. Harriet's knock was answered by a youngish maid with gold curls beneath her cap. "Mrs. Harriet Boyne. I'm here to see Miss Wraxhall, if you please."

"Sarah!" called a rough baritone voice, "If it's Mrs. Outerbridge remind her that she sees Dr. Penrose now."

Harriet nodded at Sarah as the maid stepped back and opened the door wider. A short hall led to a small parlor on the right, where Sarah made the introductions in a careful voice.

Mrs. Wraxhall had the same mouth as her daughter. She worried her lower lip as her hands worked stitches in a purse, the hook so fine it looked like a needle. Dr. Wraxhall had his son's good looks but wore them sternly, without Peter's lightness or openness. "How can I help you, Mrs. Boyne?"

Harriet put on her most presentable manners. "My friends and I have just taken possession of Thornycroft Hall, sir. Yesterday I had the good fortune"—ha—"to meet your daughter Lydia. But your family was already known to me: your son was in the same regiment as my late husband, whom I followed to the Crimea."

The doctor's eyes didn't soften in the slightest, but his wife's hands stilled. "You knew our Peter?"

27

"I did, ma'am. Please allow me to offer you my sincerest condolences for your loss."

Mrs. Wraxhall's eyes instantly went shiny with tears. Her gaze flew to a lithograph above the mantel, and Harriet's followed—oh, good God, not that picture again. A dead soldier's body dangled like a noodle beneath an equally noodlish woman, weeping in a beautiful sort of way that caused Harriet to bristle and bite back curses. *The Field of Battle*, they called it, a reproduction of a painting by the princess royal herself. Sold to benefit the Patriotic Fund.

One of the most insipid visions of the war that Harriet had ever seen. And it had pride of place here.

Dr. Wraxhall stepped forward to put a heavy hand on his wife's shoulder. The other fingered his watch-chain. "As you see, our family is not churlish in our patriotism. I like to think that in some small way, we helped Sevastopol to fall."

Harriet's face didn't move, frozen with a chill so cold it burned. She'd seen Sevastopol. The siege had begun with the ships in harbor—Harriet and Mrs. Marwood were on the *Cyclops* then. Harriet's husband was dead, and Marwood would soon follow, but not before his wife gave birth to their child as the bombardment roared around them.

It had taken nearly a year of shelling and starvation, disease and death, before the city had surrendered. Thousands of soldiers had fallen in the worst ways. Peter had died. The child had died, and Mrs. Marwood had turned her face to the sky and slipped into a six-month silence.

And for all this, Dr. Wraxhall wanted his share of credit.

He was welcome to it. His wife was still watching the lithograph. As though that amateur's reproduction of a war some princess had never seen could make up for the loss of a real and living son.

Harriet forced words out through a choked throat. "Is Miss Wraxhall in, sir?"

The doctor blinked. "Oh, I'm sure she's out back with those chickens of hers."

Harriet made as polite a farewell as she could, and escaped.

Outside again she breathed easier. She found Miss Wraxhall in the farthest corner of the back garden, beyond a turn in the carefully manicured hedges, where a wire fence separated the chicken yard from the part of the garden that was purely ornamental.

Not that the chicken yard wasn't pleasing to look at: it was a cozy patch of land, hidden at the end of the property and almost extending into the wood. Miss Wraxhall's coop was a tall six-sided cylinder, with star-shaped windows and a well-shingled roof and a weathervane in the shape of—what else—a rooster. The real rooster was close beside his mistress's dark skirts, scratching happily at the ground.

The six silvery hens from yesterday were in a wire pen in the center of the yard. The rooster occasionally wandered over to chirrup a hello, but should one of the other hens venture close the hens made warning sounds.

They made more of those sounds, even louder, as Harriet strode toward them. "You stole my chickens, Miss Wraxhall."

"I did no such thing." The woman's dark-and-silver head lifted. She smiled, utterly unconcerned over Harriet's wrath. "I lured them. They followed me because they wanted to."

Did her tongue linger a little over the vowel in *lured*? Or was Harriet simply imagining the mischievous undertone? "They followed you because you'd fed them."

"Are we meant to blame them for that?" Miss Wraxhall returned. She reached into a pocket and cast another, deliberately provocative handful of grain to the caged grey hens. "Would you rather have them starved? In winter, no less?"

"I would rather have the three hens we agreed on safe at Thornycroft Hall."

"Do you have the facilities for them?"

"Certainly," Harriet lied.

"Describe them, then."

Harriet scowled. "A small run, with a coop."

Miss Wraxhall smirked. "What kind of coop? How many birds will fit? Straw or wood shavings for litter?"

"I'm sure I don't have to tell you."

"You've no idea, do you?"

"Listen, Miss—"

Harriet bit back an angry retort, because Miss Wraxhall's expression had shuttered. The teasing light bled away, the smirk faded, the color in her cheeks now shame instead of excitement.

Harriet found she didn't like this change, not one bit.

Harriet turned at a soft sound to see Mrs. Wraxhall standing beside her, the very picture of reproach in her mourning dress, with her grey hair swooping over her ears and pinned at the nape of her neck. "Lydia, dear—your father will need you to sit with Mrs. Ramsay. Her girl has just come by to say she's taken a turn."

"Of course." Lydia's hands rubbed against her skirts, once and then again, as if trying to scrub the grain from her palms even though her hands were empty. She turned back to Harriet. "Can we continue this tomorrow, Mrs. Boyne? Your chickens will be safe here until then. *We're* not eating them."

Mrs. Wraxhall made a soft sound of reproach, but that pointed little dig sent a trickle of relief through Harriet. "Of course," she said.

Mrs. Wraxhall led her back to the front door with a stiff dignity that set Harriet's teeth on edge. She felt her spirits lighten, relieved, with every step that took her further from the house. She no longer wondered why Miss Wraxhall had chosen snow and solitude yesterday, if this was the home she had to return to.

The chickens were of course still in their pen the next afternoon. They even seemed to be curious about the other hens—or were at least making less of a fuss whenever the older birds wandered near their cage.

Miss Wraxhall, however, having just finished spreading new straw on the floor of the coop, looked rather the worse for wear, with deep bags of exhaustion under her eyes and lines of strain at the corners of her mouth.

"How is Mrs. Ramsay?" Harriet asked.

Miss Wraxhall lowered her eyes. "Not suffering any longer."

"I'm so sorry." Condolences came easily, out of habit, but not emptily: Harriet seemed to feel each death a little more than the one before, even if it was a stranger who'd died. Like they were all the same death, somehow, connected, whether it happened in an old bed beside a familiar fireplace, or in mud and misery on the far side of the world. "Do you often attend deathbeds?"

"Not as often as Father Lloyd or Dr. Penrose—but yes, as a doctor's daughter and a charitable woman of the parish, I find I can be useful when a person approaches the end. Especially in cases of people who have no family to do for them."

"I'm sure Mrs. Ramsay appreciated that."

"She was asleep when I arrived, and she never woke up."

"Still," Harriet insisted.

Miss Wraxhall's eyes narrowed. "Did you have a particular errand here today, Mrs. Boyne?"

"I've come to ask you to tea."

Miss Wraxhall's head snapped up, eyes wide. "Tea?" she blurted.

Harriet felt a smile pulling at the corners of her mouth. "At Thornycroft Hall. You can even inspect our chicken run, if you'd like. Make sure it's worthy of its promised tenants."

Miss Wraxhall stared for another moment. As if this was the first such invitation she'd ever received. When that couldn't possibly be the case. You only had to look at the woman to deduce that.

"All right," the woman said at last. "For the chickens."

They set off soon after, up the road that ribboned between the hills that bubbled between Thornycroft and the rest of the village. Harriet hadn't intended to issue the invitation, but she was glad for whatever impulse had slipped the words to her tongue.

In Harriet's experience there were two kinds of people: those who could be counted on when death came calling, and those who turned away. No wonder Dr. Wraxhall could keep a noble, romantic picture of a corpse at the center of his home: he had Miss Wraxhall to do all the unbeautiful work for when someone was actually dying. The washing of limbs, the changing of sheets, all the embarrassing, unspeakable business of a body at the end of its time. And the waiting—all those eternal hours asking yourself silently if this would be the last breath, or this one, or this.

Maybe there was more to it: maybe the good doctor had other reasons for leaving Mrs. Ramsay to his daughter's care. But somehow Harriet didn't think so.

And if you hadn't been able to help with the dying, you helped the ones who did. For instance, you could offer them tea, in a place where nobody could stick their head out the window and find another chore for them to do when they were exhausted and wrung out.

Which reminded Harriet: "May I make a confession, Miss Wraxhall?"

"Of course."

"This is the first time we've had a guest here at Thornycroft since we returned to England. My friends and I are still... It was..." Harriet stopped, and sighed, and started again. "Everyone goes to the war together—but we come back separately shattered. If you see what I mean."

"I do," Miss Wraxhall said. "I was planning to make a few remarks about the weather, and possibly ask where your friends grew up."

Harriet snorted. "Ah, the safest possible mode of conversation."

"It's not the height of wit or sophistication, I'll grant you," Miss Wraxhall returned. "But I find that if what you want is to get to know someone, the safe little questions are the most direct way to start. If someone is unpleasant to talk to about the weather, you're not going to care about their other thoughts and feelings, or want to tell them your own. The little things are a way of establishing trust: because seeing how someone behaves is a good start to learning who they are."

"And what if they break the rules of this game?" Harriet pushed. "What if someone doesn't know the patterns of polite conversation, or a question about the weather reminds them of—" she swallowed the rest of it, because if she'd kept going Harriet was suddenly afraid she would burst into tears here on a public road, where the wind whistled high and sharp and the snow-dusted hills suddenly loomed around her like stormclouds. She could feel her shoulders high and tight, bracing against the thunder her body couldn't stop expecting…

A hand on her arm. Miss Wraxhall was looking up at her. That sunlight smile was back, but fainter—a single ray rather than a summer. "It's not about setting a test and seeing if the other person can pass," she said quietly. Quietly, even though there was nobody else around for miles in any direction. "It's more like a dance—one person moves back as the other moves forward. Sometimes you both know how to waltz, but other times you have to make up the motions as you go. Can we find a rhythm together? Or are we hopelessly out of step?"

Deep within the frozen ice of Harriet's heart, something cracked, and beneath it, something hard began to melt. "I haven't danced in a very long time, Miss Wraxhall."

"A pity." The other woman's hand dropped away and tucked itself back into the muff she carried. Harriet could still feel the pressure of that touch, though, like a band wrapped around her arm. "There's usually dancing at the end of the poultry show, after all the awards have been handed out." She gasped, and delight blazed up in her eyes. "You should enter!"

Harriet blinked. "The dancing?"

"No, the poultry show."

"With what bird?"

"One of the Bickerton Greys, of course." At Harriet's scoff, Miss Wraxhall pressed on. "If what you want is to be left alone and gossiped about and seen as outsiders to the village, then that's your right and I won't try to argue with you. But if you'd like to get to know the village and become known in turn—then the quickest, best way is the Bickerton Christmas Poultry Show." Her eyes took on a sharp glitter, like her thoughts had turned serrated. "And what's more, I bet you could win."

"Oh yes," Harriet muttered. "Because what country village doesn't appreciate a new arrival turning up and showing off? They're sure to like me then."

The doctor's daughter waved this aside. "It's not about making them like you. You have the whole rest of the year for that. It's about showing that you are a part of the life of this place."

Miss Wraxhall's eyes were on the road, her pace increasing, as though the excitement of the idea were translating to the speed of her feet. Harriet's longer legs meant she had no trouble keeping up—but it was surprising how enjoyable the stretch of it felt. They covered the rest of the way in no time at all, as Miss Wraxhall described the way to prepare a chicken for show—which Harriet was too charmed by to interrupt, even though she didn't bother to try and remember it all.

At Thornycroft, Mrs. Goodfellow was sewing in the parlor while Mrs. Crangle wrote up a list of the coming week's necessary supplies. The latter leapt up at once to offer tea when Harriet made introductions. Mrs. Goodfellow hopped up, a few blonde wisps of hair escaping their pins, and offered Miss Wraxhall the seat closest to the fire. Mr. Dixit drifted down, lured by the smell of scones and butter, and the party was complete.

Miss Wraxhall was warm and polite and not the least bit intrusive; before long Lizzie was telling tales of the tavern she'd run in Brighton before the war—no surprise, as Lizzie was a chatty sort. Harriet even relaxed enough to offer the story of the first disastrous holiday after her wedding, and Mr. Dixit described the cases in some of the letters he was writing.

Harriet looked over to see how Miss Wraxhall was taking this in—and saw that the poor woman, well fed and warm and cozied up in one of Mrs. Goodfellow's quilts, had fallen helplessly asleep. Lizzie chuckled, assured Mr. Dixit he was not at all dull, and retrieved the empty teacup before it could fall from their guest's slack hand.

"She was up all night at someone's deathbed," Harriet explained.

Lizzie nodded understanding, and Arun's anxious expression softened. Mrs. Goodfellow tapped a finger against her lips. They slipped out of the room and back to their usual occupations.

Harriet, after a moment, picked up a book and settled into the other fireside chair. She had only intended to let Miss Wraxhall sleep a few moments—but the book was better than she expected, and the time escaped her. She had just met the cold Mr. Thornton, clearly the villain of the piece, when a quiet sound from the other chair reminded her she was not in Milton, but in her own parlor.

"Miss Wraxhall?" Harriet murmured.

The woman made that sound again, a little creak from the back of her throat. Her eyes were still closed and her lips slightly parted.

Harriet leaned closer. There were still the dark marks of exhaustion beneath Miss Wraxhall's eyes: Harriet fought the temptation to press her fingertips to the skin there and try to smooth them away. She looked younger when asleep, as the fine lines at the corners of her eyes and mouth eased a little, free of their tension and movement. One wayward lock of Miss Wraxhall's hair, twined silver and sable, was resting against her cheekbone.

This time, temptation won.

Harriet's fingers gently brushed that lock of hair back and tucked it behind one sweetly curling ear.

Miss Wraxhall's eyes flew open.

Harriet's breath was sucked from her lungs. She froze, staring into those rich brown eyes. Something soft and warm flickered there, just for a moment, and Harriet's spine ached with the strain

35

of not leaning forward and seeing if Miss Wraxhall's lips were as soft and sweet as they looked.

Instead, she sat back in her own chair and put her hands firmly around the book, where they could get into no mischief. "You're awake," she said.

Miss Wraxhall yawned and rubbed at the side of her neck. Her voice was still sleep-muffled, velvet and warm. "I'm so sorry, I've never done that before."

Harriet's pulse jumped, and her knuckles whitened where they held the novel. "You seemed like you needed the rest," she said gruffly.

Miss Wraxhall's lips flattened with chagrin. "I hope you made my apologies to your friends. It was rude of me, and no mistake— and after all those things I told you about polite conversation."

"And dancing," Harriet added.

One corner of her mouth tweaked. "And dancing."

Harriet had to look away. She'd not been this distracted and compelled by someone since—well, since John. She'd thought that part of her had died, stomped into the mud of Balaklava and frozen over with a forever winter. Spring was coming again, an appalling surprise. She flailed for something to say. "Would you like to see our chicken run?"

It was the right thing, apparently. Miss Wraxhall beamed. "Naturally."

3

The Thornycroft Hall chicken run was spacious and solid and needed only a good scouring before the three Bickerton Greys could take possession. Lydia agonized the entire night before, but ultimately she could not bear to split the feral flock and so all six wound up leaving Lydia's cozy coop and moving into the hutch built against the stately grey stone walls at Thornycroft. "Just remember," she said, "three of them are mine."

Mrs. Boyne snorted. "Which three?"

"The best three."

Mrs. Boyne laughed outright at this, as Lydia had hoped.

It was hard to stay formal when fowl were involved. They were Harriet and Lydia by the end of the first week. Now the only thing was to accustom the wild birds to the presence and handling of humans. Dusty, scratchy birds took home no awards —and Lydia was determined to show these birds at their best.

The hens resisted: Bickerton Greys were intelligent enough to be wary, and these hens had been defending themselves from predators for all their lives. Lydia eventually decided to move Walter to Thornycroft as well, as a sort of poultry ambassador. Shockingly, the tactic worked, and one clear day the hens permitted themselves to be washed.

It was a wintry dazzle. Tubs with soapy water and clean steamed in the air, silver-laced plumage sparkled in the sharp November sun, and the flock bustled around Walter like a sextet of pearls around a ruby.

"They need names," Lydia said.

"Hmm?" Harriet raised her head from her book: she had brought a wooden bench into the yard and often sat there, reading and letting the birds grow familiar with her presence. "Will they know their names?"

"Of course."

Harriet shrugged. "Alright." She raised a gloved hand, elegant as any queen, and began pointing. "One, Two, Three, Four, Five, and Six."

Lydia rolled her eyes. "Astonishing. Absolutely astonishing."

"Alright: Monday, Tuesday, Wednesday—"

"Now you're just listing ordinary things!"

Harriet grinned. "You try it, then."

Lydia scrutinized the little flock, the six guardian Greys and the tall red rooster in the middle. A shadow flickered over the yard—a sense of swooping wings—and the hens as one bunched up around Walter, a clear defensive formation that, just as clearly, puzzled him.

Lydia began pointing. "Boudicca, Joan, Minerva, Atalanta, Camilla, Penthesilea."

Harriet snorted. *"Penthesilea?"*

"Penny for short, if you'd like."

Lydia grinned, as Harriet very visibly refused to rise to the bait of this provocation. The widow watched the birds, who had relaxed as the bird overhead moved on without incident.

They were a very managing breed, Lydia had realized; she also realized that she found it rather endearing.

Harriet asked, "Which ones will do best in the show, in your expert opinion?"

Lydia considered this. "Boudicca and Minerva have the best plumage. Minerva especially: the lacing is so sharp and the color contrast is strongest." She cocked a head, watching as the birds milled about Walter, nudging him for attention. "But Penny has the best shape overall, I think."

Harriet's eyes were narrowed, one hand raised to her forehead for shade as she watched the birds. "How do you judge a breed that's supposed to not exist anymore?"

"We can find an old catalog of the points somewhere, I'm sure. Mr. Finglass has a collection." Lydia sat beside her on the bench. "Besides, it's only been ten years—Mrs. Outerbridge alone has grudges that are twice and three times as old as that. Someone will remember the last time the breed was shown, and will not hesitate to tell us how our bird compares to the ideal."

Harriet poked her with a gentle elbow. "Our bird, is it now?"

Lydia toed the dust, watching Walter bustle about and make happy sounds to his hens. "Don't tell me you've kept track of which three are yours, and which mine?"

"I'm sure I don't care. I don't even care about winning the prize, to be perfectly frank."

Lydia scowled. "Well, I do!"

"Then it's a good thing your Walter is so beautiful, isn't it?"

Lydia scowled harder. He wasn't entirely her Walter anymore, either. He had settled in here at Thornycroft with the Grey hens as if he owned the manor outright. Mrs. Crangle snuck him tidbits and called him delicious—which had slightly alarmed Lydia, until she learned it was simply Mrs. Crangle's highest form of praise— and he occasionally fluttered up to the bench and into Harriet's lap while she read. It was only Lydia who had to make the long, lonely walk back down through the hills at the end of every day.

She was starting to have to make excuses to visit.

Harriet and Mrs. Crangle and the staff had the birds' everyday care well in hand by now, so Lydia had had suggested bathing the chickens—so it wouldn't come as a shock to the hens when they were washed and fluffed for show the week before Christmas. But this wasn't something they could do every day—even if Lydia had wanted to, which quite frankly she didn't—and soon she

39

feared she would have to stretch her imagination for more and more outlandish pretexts.

The coop would be better with a second story.

We should train the chickens to sing.

Any day I don't see you is a day wasted.

Ridiculous, this yearning.

The hens had dried and were back to their usual explorations, so Harriet and Lydia returned to the kitchen, where Mrs. Crangle was just pulling a glossy, glowing pigeon pie from the oven. Harriet claimed it, procured a pot of tea, and lured Lydia to the parlor.

Lydia was three forkfuls deep when a new face appeared in the doorway.

She was a small woman with soft brown hair, creamy skin, and the saddest eyes Lydia had ever seen. "Harriet, did Mary ask you —oh," she said. "I'm sorry, I didn't mean to…"

Lydia swallowed her pie and smiled apologetically.

The woman's eyes went even wider, and her face went marble-white.

Harriet was up at once, putting a hand under the woman's elbow. "Ellie, this is Miss Lydia Wraxhall," she said.

Her voice was gentler and more careful than Lydia had ever heard it. The quiet pond of Lydia's jealousy gave a ripple, as if a stone had been tossed into it, and not a small one.

"Lydia," Harriet said, and there was a worry and a warning in her eyes, "this is Eleanor Marwood."

Oh. *Oh.* Over a year since Lydia had read that name, in the last letter her brother had written home. *My great good friend Marwood is gone,* he'd said. It was one of their old code phrases they'd used growing up, so they could talk safely about things their parents did not want to understand. *Great good friend* meant *the man I love.* The ink on the line had been lightly smeared, as if Peter had hurriedly wiped away a tear before it could blot the page further.

And the line that followed: *His widow is expecting.*

Eleanor Marwood had been in camp, with the army. Had she

known? Peter had been careful, but he was so transparent where he loved. How could anyone not have known?

And now the small woman looked stricken, shocked to the bone. Harriet guided her to the chair and hovered beside her. "You look so much like him," Mrs. Marwood said faintly.

"I will take that as a compliment," Lydia replied.

Mrs. Marwood nodded. "You should," she said, her voice firming. A light had come into her eyes. "Your brother saved my life. And he was gone before I could thank him for it. I owe your family a great debt, Miss Wraxhall."

Lydia flushed. "I'm sure Peter would not want you to feel you owe us anything, Mrs. Marwood."

The widow chewed her lip. "I'm sorry, I didn't think—does it pain you to talk of him?"

"No. Well, yes—but I'd still like to do it. Will you..." Lydia swallowed. "Will you tell me about him? He'd been away for so many years, you see—we had his letters, plenty of them, but he was never any good at seeing himself as he truly was."

Mrs. Marwood nodded at that. "He was very hard on himself. Needlessly hard. I don't think I've ever met anyone else who worked so hard at being good. Your parents must have been very proud."

The pang that went through Lydia was an old one, but still sharp. "They are very proud to have a soldier in the family," she managed, though her throat was thick.

Mrs. Marwood was watching her closely. "A soldier, not a son?"

Lydia flushed. "My father always hoped Peter would take up his practice after him. My mother wanted grandchildren. Peter wanted neither of those futures. It made things... tense, at times." Mrs. Marwood's quiet, gentle gaze invited confidences, so Lydia found herself adding: "I think they found it much easier to be proud of him at a distance."

"You mean they liked the idea of a son more than the son himself," Harriet said, with a frown.

41

Lydia's flushed deepened, a painful red burn on her cheeks. "I wouldn't say so."

"Marwood's family were much the same," the widow went on. "He thought if he got married it would make them happy."

"Did it not?" Lydia asked, taking a sip of her tea.

Mrs. Marwood shook her head. "Maybe if he'd married the girl they thought he should." Her mouth quirked. "Maybe if he'd stopped falling in love with men."

Lydia choked. Tea went in all the wrong places in her throat, and it was a long time before she could cough her way clear again and wipe the moisture from her eyes.

Mrs. Marwood was laughing silently, her whole self transformed by it. "Oh, I do enjoy shocking people. And I have so few opportunities for it these days. Thank you for that, Miss Wraxhall." Then, as quick as it had come, her mirth vanished. She rose and nodded and drifted out again, sadness wreathing her like a queenly mantle.

Harriet watched her anxiously. "That was the longest conversation we've had from her in months. Of all of us, she left the most behind her in Crimea. You ought to have seen her as she was—she and your brother were very much of a type."

"I see." Lydia fingered the handle of her teacup, fussing with the porcelain and using it as a distraction. Mrs. Marwood's little bombshell had opened certain possibilities in the conversation. Confession would be a relief—but it was a risk, too. "Peter and I…" Lydia started, and stopped, took a breath, and all but flung the words out. "Peter and I used to joke that someone had switched our hearts. Because he had eyes only for men, and I was forever drawn to women."

"Ah," Harriet breathed. Barely a sound, almost a sigh.

"That's why he joined the army. It was a penance for an ineradicable flaw. He wanted to do all he could to make up for it, you see."

"And the army doesn't let an officer marry without permission," Harriet added.

Lydia nodded. "So all he had to do was never ask permission. And our parents' arguments lost purchase. Especially when he talked of the nobility of soldiering, though I'm not certain he truly believed all he said."

Harriet snorted. "Nobility of war wears off quicker than the polish on a new soldier's boot." She bit her lip, eyes far away—then suddenly she leaned forward, the shift in intensity pinning Lydia in place like a rapier, sliding through her with almost no pain at all. "I have known war. I have seen the grief it brings, seen people use that grief like a knife to wound themselves and others. Your brother took that weapon and made it into a shield. He protected a widow and her child until his last breath left his lungs, for the love of a man he'd already lost. He stole food for them, he found them clothing and shelter when everything was rags and mud. He used his last strength to write a letter for us to take to Lady Eccleston, to get us away from the war at last. Because a man he loved would have wanted him to." Harriet's voice caught; she choked the emotion back and went ruthlessly on. "You cannot tell me a love like that is anything short of holy, or anything less than a miracle, when it felt like a blessing just to have seen it. The kind of vision that would give a sinner the unshakeable faith of a saint. A love like a bonfire—or a sun. I don't care what the laws say, or what the church claims God decrees. I have learned there is something better than all that, and I hope—" She let out a laugh like a sob. "I hope someday to have a chance to throw my own cold heart headlong into the flames."

The anguish in her voice nearly broke Lydia. It felt old, hardened, scarred over. Lydia knew what it felt like to yearn for love, to pine for desire, lonely but more than lonely because you knew what you were missing. Ashes that remembered what it felt like to burn.

Lydia had spent the last ten years seeing the same small people in this small town over and over. Her heart had already tested itself on everyone local. Love had flared, then faded into comfortable friendships. She'd believed she'd only find love again if she left Bickerton, but she had been too cowardly to leave. It was daunting, to uproot an entire life—especially for a love you could never name outside of stolen whispers. Especially when her parents had already lost one child: her clear duty was to comfort them in her brother's place.

And now Harriet Boyne had come, a widow whose spine was ice and her mouth blood-red, those lips forming words that spoke to the deepest longing of Lydia's own heart.

I would love you, if you let me. The words filled her mouth like honey.

"You must have loved your husband," she said instead.

"I did," Harriet confirmed. "And he loved me. But he wanted to love me at a distance. The way your parents love your brother. He wanted to love a wife, but not a person." She slumped back in her chair, shoulders curving with an old burden of hurt. "I read the early reports of the war and couldn't stand being so many miles and months away. I followed him out—and found he'd rather I'd have stayed at home."

"Perhaps he wanted to protect you."

Lydia's hand tightened on the arm of the chair, knuckles white beneath taut skin. "He told me I'd only made a burden of myself. The army makes no provision for its soldiers' wives on campaign. They are given no rations, no equipment, not even funds with which to buy food. The French do things differently—they have many of their women acting as sutlers, in uniform. Very brave and bright beside our ragged English wives. Well, I had known I'd have to make my own way, but I thought at least John would welcome me. Instead, we fought. Bitterly. I offered him a sacrifice he had no use for. 'Well good riddance to him, and good riddance to love!' I thought. I would have shipped home the next day—but there was no homebound ship to take me, and no living for me there but what I could scrape. And then Alma came, and John was gone." Her voice was hard as stone now, cold as ice. "I was then offered a widow's pension. You see, John had done it properly and obtained his commanding officer's approval." She fidgeted

44

and sat up, her spine and shoulders stiff and haughty. "The army will grant us a living or a living husband, but never both at once."

Lydia's hands ached to reach out in comfort. "I'm astonished you can still talk of love after that."

Harriet shrugged. "I'd bought myself a diamond and found it to be paste," she replied. "But I know true gems exist. I only wish…" She stopped.

Lydia stared. Harriet Boyne looking anxious was a rare thing. She didn't like it. "What do you wish?"

Harriet sucked in a breath. Her eyes had gone chilly again, bleak as the winter world outside. "I wish I didn't have to explain so much. About John, about the war. About myself, really. I wish I could just—*feel* something other than broken." She shook her head. "Indoors I chafe at confinement, and outdoors I feel small and lonely. I can put it out of my mind for a little while," as she stroked a grateful hand over the cover of her latest novel, "but I don't want to spend the rest of my life trying to escape from myself. I just—don't know what else to do."

The plaintive confession, plainly spoken, all but broke Lydia's heart. She had never been to war, had never lost a husband—but she knew that lonely restlessness far too well. And she realized: she'd offered to help Harriet become part of the life of Bickerton— but maybe also she'd hoped to escape. Her own life had started to feel far too small, bounded by rules that cut tighter and tighter as the years marched on. Thornycroft was just far enough away from the rest of Bickerton that it felt like a separate place. Another world.

In fact, Lydia remembered, it had felt like that before. On one particular night, long ago, after Lady Eccleston's year of morning for her father ended.

Lydia leaned forward. "Harriet, have you seen Thornycroft Hall's ballroom?"

᠃ ᠃ ᠃ ᠃

Harriet had known the ballroom was there, of course. It was hard to overlook such a space. But the heirs of Thornycroft Hall had the opposite of interest in throwing a ball now or any time in future, so they had left it closed up the way they'd first found it.

Now Harriet found herself pushing open the double doors and slipping inside, Lydia hot on her heels.

It was a vast cave of a space, a jewel-box lozenge with a parquet floor and a small gallery along one of the long sides. Drop cloths made craggy boulders of stored tables and chairs, as well as the distinctive shape of a piano against the wall beneath the gallery. A few trunks of stored things had found their way here as well, unwelcome in the rest of the house.

Lydia made for the windows, where daylight was leaking in at the edges of the drapes. She began pulling the fabric aside, and one by one the two-story stretches of glass were cleared to pour sharp sunlight into the room. With the brightness outside and the dimness inside, Thornycroft's view of rolling hills and snow-dusted woods was sliced into a series of landscapes—as though some great mural artist had painted them specially for the delight of the guests who had come to dance.

Lydia brushed the dust from her hands and fixed the curtain ties in place. "There. How's that?"

Harriet blinked, and considered. There really were a great many windows—she walked over to the one Lydia stood near, and could feel the winter's chill leaching through, cooling the air nearest the panes. She could see the length of fully half the property, and even the top of the steeple of St. Gilbert's, the highest point in Bickerton half a mile away. Yet at the same time she felt protected, buttressed in some wordless way by the knowledge that the house, with all its stone and wood and weight, waited at her back. Space and shelter, inside and outside were no longer opposites, but met in peaceful accord.

She turned to Lydia. "You've been here before."

"I was twenty." Lydia's cheeks flushed, and her smile was full of secrets. "Lady Eccleston gave a ball—her first since her father's

46

death the year before. All her high-born London friends came down, and all the families in the neighborhood were invited. Peter got all his friends to ask me to dance—but I slipped away to the gallery, because Jane Arbuthnot was up there and I had to see the what candlelight looked like in her hair."

Harriet could see it: Lydia coltish and eager, hope sparkling like a star in her eyes. Candles would tint the whole room gold and turn the windows into dark mirrors. This place would be a kaleidoscope of colorful silk and dazzling gems. And in the gallery, two girls, breathless with desire. Harriet moved a step closer. "Did you kiss her?"

"Jane?" Lydia's laugh was rueful, a sound of pity for her past self. "Jane only had eyes for Roger de Voy. She married him six months later."

"And broke your heart."

Lydia laughed again—defiantly this time. "By then I was sneaking out every night to meet Emily Inch beneath the apple tree." She pursed her lips, smug with memory. "She *did* kiss me, Emily did."

That defiant laugh fluttered beneath Harriet's fingertips as she rested them lightly on the side of Lydia's throat. Lydia caught her breath, her dark eyes wide with surprise. Harriet moved slowly, giving Lydia time to pull away as she leaned forward.

Lydia met her halfway there.

Memory tasted sweet on Lydia's lips. Harriet wanted more: her hand curved around the nape of Lydia's neck and pulled her closer. Their tongues tangled, and Lydia let out a soft moan that Harriet instantly devoured.

It was greedy of her, she knew. Lydia deserved the kiss she'd sought that night, a memory wrapped in silk and candlelight. All Harriet could offer was this pale imitation, a flash of wintry silver glinting off ice.

And Harriet, starved as she was, wanted more. She scraped her teeth against the swell of Lydia's lower lip. "Did you ever do more than kiss?"

Lydia's laugh was a puff of breath, warm where it tickled over Harriet's cheek. "You have been away too long, if you think English country girls have forgotten how to fuck."

Harriet's pulse leapt. "Even proper doctor's daughters?"

Lydia leaned in, voice low and heated, her lips moving against the delicate skin of Harriet's jaw. "What could be more proper than two girls—two very good friends—taking long walks together in the summer?" Lydia teased. "Or spending hours in a bedroom, trading gowns and gossip? No doubt they're only sharing secrets when they bend their heads close together, arm in arm. And if they come down to the parlor rosier than they went up, with knees that wobble a little on the stairs—well, that's just feminine weakness and overexcitement, isn't it. Nothing to worry over. A little rest, and she'll soon be the picture of good health."

Harriet chuckled. "You wanton."

Lydia leaned back, eyes considering. "Are you telling me this is the first time you've kissed a woman?" That smugness was back; Harriet liked it on her. "Didn't feel like the first time."

"Unlike you, I never pretended to be proper," Harriet answered. Her fingers were tracing Lydia's cheekbone, moving from freckle to freckle, shaping constellations over velvet skin. "I kissed anyone I could catch. And a bit more, sometimes. My parents almost despaired of me—until John proposed." Her fingers stilled, and her heart made a fist in her throat.

Lydia's hand caught hers, lacing comforting fingers with Harriet's. "I admire your recklessness," she said. "It was easy for me, being invisible. Maybe if my parents hadn't been so busy scrutinizing Peter, they'd have noticed more of the things I was up to."

Harriet grazed one more kiss over her mouth, distracting them both from that particular branch of thought. "I want to hear all of your secret exploits," she murmured, making Lydia part her lips on a silent laugh. "Stay for dinner?"

Lydia's shy smile was at odds with the heat in her eyes. "Of course."

Harriet was so pleased by this, she reached for more. "Stay the night?"

Lydia dimmed. Winter light made her profile icy as she turned to regard the road home. "I don't know if my parents can spare me."

Harriet shouldn't push. She shouldn't be disappointed; she knew how it could be, trying to make yourself important to someone who was important to you. But the thought of Lydia being trapped in that little house, with its crepe and its sadness and its cold corpse paintings, was nearly unbearable. "Dinner, then," she said, trying to console them both.

~ ~ ~ ~

Dinner was utterly ordinary. Lydia, Harriet, Mrs. Crangle, Mr. Dixit, and Mrs. Goodfellow sat at the table; Mrs. Marwood had a plate brought up to her in her room. The food was plain and plentiful; the conversation trivial; the fire crackling in the hearth was merely a way of keeping warm.

It was one of the best nights of Lydia's life.

She stole one more lingering kiss when Harriet walked her to the door, but then it was out into the night and the dark and the cold.

The hills loomed on either side, snow-dusted. The sky above was clouded, hiding the stars. Lydia's breath puffed into the air, and her chest grew lighter with every step she took back toward Bickerton. By now her parents would have eaten, but they wouldn't have gone to bed. One of them always sat up until she returned—her mother crocheting by lamplight, her father with a book. A blanket over their shoulders, as the fire burned down to embers. And no relief when Lydia returned, only impatience that she'd kept them so long from their rest.

Never mind that she'd never asked them to wait up. Never mind that she was past forty, that Bickerton was a sleepy rural village not notably beset by thieves and murderers, that Lydia had spent the greater part of her life fulfilling every duty her parents could think to ask from her. Never mind, too, that she wasn't always sure they loved her except as a vaguely daughter-shaped thing that belonged to them.

The thought flared resentfully, as she watched a single snowflake pirouette out of the leaden sky.

If only there were more of them. A flurry, a whole blizzard of white flakes, sweet as sugar. They were past due for this decade's storm. A real tempest, that would send her back to Thornycroft for shelter—for warmth—into Harriet's arms and Harriet's parted lips—

She stopped abruptly, her feet frozen to the road.

Safety. Was that the only thing she was permitted to ask for? Here she was praying for a blizzard, for the risk of dying in the cold, because it made the choice to go back to Harriet a matter of *safety*. What about wanting? What about happiness? Why wasn't she allowed—no, why wasn't she *allowing herself* to choose what she wanted, simply because she wanted it?

Who was really holding her back?

It wasn't her parents, she could see that now. They would be cross if she stayed out all night—but what of that? Would they love her less? If so, then their love meant nothing. If not, what was the risk?

She'd been thinking of Bickerton—possibly all her life—as a place where there was no opportunity for courage. As though she had to be the cautious one, the fearful one, because Peter had been brave. She'd been trying to make up for his loss by being everything he wasn't.

How foolish. She couldn't heal the loss of her brother, even if her parents saw her for who she wanted to be: Peter's death was a separate wound, a hurt that would always hurt. Not something she had to atone for, or a debt she had to repay.

All she was doing was wasting her own time. Her own life—not a day more of which was guaranteed. She could choke on a morsel of food, she could be struck down by one of any number of sudden maladies, or be mowed down by a runaway coach in the high street. She could—she glanced up at the sky—let herself freeze to death standing stock still in the middle of a road she'd traveled a hundred times or more, because she was so existentially flummoxed by her own idiocy.

She turned her back on Bickerton and started moving again.

The walk was even more agonizing now, her impatience making a quarter-mile feel like an endless trudge. But at last she emerged from the hills to see Thornycroft Hall ahead. Candles winked in a few of its windows on the upper story—Mrs. Marwood and Mr. Dixit, if she had to guess—but Lydia was drawn around to the right, where the ballroom loomed like a high and icy hall, with a single star flickering in its depths.

Lydia crunched across the stone patio and rapped at the glass door.

It was a long, breathless moment—but then Harriet was there, on the glass's other side, a lonely taper in her hand and a look of astonishment in her eyes.

Lydia grinned, and gave a little wave.

Harriet pulled the door open with some effort and a screech of old hinges that ought to have killed all the romance in the air. "Am I dreaming?" she whispered, then shivered at the draft. "Aren't you cold?"

"Not anymore," Lydia said, and reached for her.

Harriet grasped her cold hands before they could touch skin. "Yes you are," she said, sounding peevish, but failing to keep the smile from her lips. She pulled Lydia over the threshold, and pushed the protesting door shut.

Lydia stared up at the ceiling, where painted angels fluttered just out of reach of the light. She still held all her newfound bravery in her hands, but didn't know where to put it. Harriet raised a single eyebrow. "I changed my mind," Lydia said.

"I gathered that," Harriet replied dryly.

Lydia turned and looked at her. "You changed your clothes."

At dinner Harriet had been wearing a gown of deep burgundy

OLIVIA WAITE

wool in the stark and elegant lines she favored. Her night-dress was flannel, practical as Lydia might have guessed. But over it she'd put on a dressing gown of what could only be silk, blue-green with embroidered birds that fluttered life-size at the hem and vanished into pinpricks at the bust and shoulders. Deep-piled velvet in the same hue lined the cuffs and the long collar piece.

It was a luscious, extravagant garment that was made to be admired. "Expecting someone special?" Lydia murmured.

Harriet blushed beneath the scrutiny, and raised her chin. "How many years has it been since you danced here, Miss Wraxhall?"

"A decade at least."

Harriet set her candle on the shrouded piano, and held out one hand.

Lydia went willingly.

She was stiff from the cold and out of practice, but how could that matter when she was in Harriet's arms, following her lead in the steps of a reel only half-remembered. The sparkle of diamonds was nothing to the glint of moonlight on snow, and no well-tuned orchestra easier to dance to than the old sad song Harriet began to help them both find a rhythm:

She raised her head from her down-soft pillow,
And snowy were her milk-white breasts,
Saying: 'Who's there, who's there at my bedroom window
Disturbing me from my long night's rest?'
''Tis I, your love, but don't discover,
I pray you rise and let me in
For I am fatigued from my long night's journey
Besides, I am wet unto my skin.'

•   •   •

52

The moonlight wasn't ice now—it was silver, and struck Lydia's heart like a bell as two pairs of feet shuffled softly over the parquet in perfect unison.

Harriet continued:

Then oh cock, oh cock, oh handsome cockerel,
I pray you not crow until it is day,
For your wings I'll make of the very first beaten gold
And your comb I'll make of the silver grey.

"Take me upstairs," Lydia whispered against Harriet's throat.

The song faltered as Harriet gasped, then laughed, a breathy sound soft as the wind outside.

She gathered her taper and they crept up to the upper story, to a bedroom at the end of the hall whose windows looked out on the abbey ruins. A banked fire kept away the worst of the chill, but Lydia was glad there was still moonlight and stone. This was not a cage, not a place set apart or hidden from the world: it was the heart of everything.

Harriet's hands became busy with her buttons, and Lydia forgot about the view outside.

Lydia hadn't taken someone to bed since before crinolines were in style, and she marveled at how relieved she felt when the thing was shed and she could press herself against Harriet with only scant layers of linen between. Kisses were heated, but hunger burned hotter. They shivered and stripped and all but dove beneath the blankets, Harriet nipping at Lydia's shoulder as she wrapped her arms around her waist.

Lydia shook at the feel of skin on skin and yelped as Harriet's chill fingertips stroked low on her belly, then lower still between her legs.

"Sorry," Harriet murmured, sounding not sorry at all. "Do you want my hand? Or my mouth?"

53

"Both?"

Harriet laughed. She sucked two fingers into her mouth, slicking them and warming them, and then her hand was back at Lydia's entrance and those fingers were slipping into Lydia and all the stars in the sky fell and burst behind her eyelids.

Lydia groaned, falling back, fighting the blankets to spread her legs wider so she could take more. Harriet leaned over, hand working with a lazy, determined rhythm that was bound to drive Lydia mad. When she leaned lower still and swirled a tongue over Lydia's nipple, Lydia fisted the sheets in her hands and cursed.

Harriet's laugh was a caress on her collarbone; her hand a piston; her mouth silken and hot as it slipped down Lydia's quivering belly. She nipped once at Lydia's hip, just a tease—and then her tongue was parting Lydia's slickened flesh and finding the hard, hot little center and stroking in time with the relentless motion of her hand. "Do that again," Lydia begged. "Deeper… harder—please…" Everything she asked for Harriet gave, and more, and it was eons or maybe seconds later that Lydia cried out and the world shivered apart.

Afterward, she ebbed back into herself, pulling in what felt like the deepest breath she'd taken in years. "Seems like you needed that," Harriet murmured. She'd only come partway back up the bed, her head pillowed against Lydia's side.

"You have no idea." Lydia stroked a hand into Harriet's hair, chestnut and silver slipping against her fingers, then locking tight as Lydia gripped it—not hard, but with insistence, a gentle fist at the back of her neck. "And you? What is it that you need?"

"Oh," Harriet said airily. "I'll take anything."

"Will you now?" Oh, if that wasn't a sentence to tempt a good English girl to resurrect her best debaucheries. Desire flooded back in, and Lydia pulled harder on Harriet's hair. "Up with you," she said sternly.

From the catch in Harriet's breath, that was the right tone to take. Lydia dropped her hand to Harriet's hips and guided her up, so that soon Lydia was flat on her back and Harriet—tall, proud Harriet, with a flush running down her neck to the top of her lovely breasts, and her hair thoroughly mussed by Lydia's hand—was kneeling with her thighs on either side of Lydia's head.

"Hold still," Lydia said.

She took her time to settle the coverlet around her feet for warmth, and a pillow plumped beneath her head for comfort. Then she looked at where Harriet's lovely pussy was waiting, just inches away, and licked her lips.

Harriet, watching, shivered.

"Cold?" Lydia drawled.

"A little," Harriet breathed. "But I like it."

Lydia had suspected she might. The embers from the hearth limned one side of her in gold, but the other was silvered with moonlight pouring in the windows. Lydia herself wanted to be wrapped in warmth—to be seized, gripped, pinned, held, and pressed down by the weight of a whole other person. But for Harriet—she remembered their conversation in the ballroom, about walls and fields and feeling trapped. Trying to fit your heart into a cage could hurt, when your heart kept beating against the bars to get out. "Put your hands on the headboard," she said. "And hold on."

As soon as Harriet gripped the wood, Lydia raised her head and feasted.

Harriet gasped, but Lydia barely heard her. Her whole world was in her mouth: sweet slickness, warm skin, softly curling hair against her cheeks. Her palms pressed Harriet's thighs wider as she licked, tonguing her with abandon and chasing every throb and pulse to its source. She'd always enjoyed this, but tonight it felt like a sharp and urgent need—to feel Harriet's flesh yield beneath her mouth and hands, to feel her thighs shake, to look up and see Harriet had pressed one hand against her mouth to muffle the series of keening cries Lydia could feel even down so low on her body.

She surfaced briefly. "If you want to make noise, I would be delighted."

Harriet squeaked and shivered, but shook her head. "Mr. Dixit might hear," she gasped. "He—he doesn't do well—with strange noises at night."

"Then we shan't disturb him." She shifted, rising to her knees in the bed. "Turn around for me, won't you?"

Harriet nodded desperately, and soon Lydia was pressed up against her back, both of them facing the window with its expanse of winter wildness. Lydia put one hand up—gently—over Harriet's mouth, and slid the other around a hip and between her thighs. Two fingers easily slipped into the heat there, and Harriet's hips began rolling insistently, hungrily. "That's good," Lydia purred into her ear. "Show me how quiet you can be."

Harriet was panting for breath, hot puffs of air against Lydia's palm. Her hips and Lydia's fingers made a whisper of wet sound as Harriet chased her pleasure. Lydia held on as she bucked, the rhythm growing wild as the ecstasy approached.

Lydia leaned forward near her ear. "Remember," she said. "Not a sound. Not a single cry—or else they'll know you're being fucked. They'll know how hard you can come after getting your pussy licked, around someone's fingers. *My* fingers."

She punctuated the last phrase by speeding up her strokes— just a hair, but it was enough. Harriet fell to pieces in her arms, muscles straining tight and her head thrown back against Lydia's shoulder.

Afterward, wrapped in a cocoon of warmth and satiety, Lydia's last thought before drifting into sleep was: whatever trouble this night brought, it was more than worth it.

4

———————

*H*arriet couldn't remember the last time she'd been lucky enough to wake up in somebody's arms. She'd forgotten how much she craved it, and Lydia seemed inclined to agree. She didn't spend every night at Thornycroft after that first time—perhaps one in every three—but she always seemed as eager to stay as Harriet was to have her, and as reluctant to leave on the nights when Harriet knew they'd be separated.

The weeks before the Poultry Fair flew by, and then it was the day before Christmas Eve, and Lydia and Harriet and Mrs. Crangle and the staff were all up before dawn to prepare. By the time the winter sun peeked its lazy head above the horizon, Harriet and Lydia were driving toward Bickerton with a cart full of willow-work cages, clean straw, and even cleaner chickens.

A spacious tent had been set up on the green across from St. Gilbert's: workmen were fixing the tent-poles in place. As soon as they entered the tent, a dozen pairs of eyes swiveled up and pinned them in place.

Harriet froze, surprised by the wash of hostility.

Lydia paid them no attention, but carted the cage with Walter and Boudicca (who had developed something of a particular tendre) over to a space on the end of a center row—central, but room to the side for them to do any work needed. One by one they moved the cages from the cart to the tent—but the animosity in all those watching pairs of eyes only grew.

Finally, all the chickens were in place, and the cages labeled neatly with each bird's breed and class. Harriet was pinning the last label in place on Minerva and Joan when a stern voice spoke from behind her. "Does that say Bickerton Grey?"

Harriet turned to see an older woman regarding her with endless suspicion—as though Harriet had offered her a cup of tea sweetened with arsenic. "It does," Harriet confirmed.

The woman shook her head, setting feathers bobbing. Harriet had the sudden wild horror that those feathers had been plucked from past champion chickens. "Bickerton Greys don't exist anymore," she said staunchly. "Not for this past decade, at least."

"Not in the village, Mrs. Outerbridge, you're right about that," Lydia said. She stood at Harriet's other elbow, smiling in a pointed, too-bright kind of way. "We found these birds in the woods—you know as well as I do that there's always been rumored sightings, a few birds thought to have survived in the wild."

"Hmph." The older woman sniffed. "And I suppose you think they're a shoo-in for the top prizes."

Lydia's smile broadened, and she waved her hand toward Boudicca and Minerva. "See for yourself."

Mrs. Outerbridge bent to peer into the cages. The hens bristled back at her with nearly identical expressions of displeasure.

Harriet bit her lip to keep from laughing.

"Have you met Mrs. Boyne yet?" Lydia said, smooth as butter. "She's one of the new owners of Thornycroft Hall."

Mrs. Outerbridge straightened. "Charmed," she said, and shook hands in a perfunctory sort of way.

Harriet got the impression her attention was still mostly on the chickens, even if she weren't looking that way at the moment.

"And what birds will you be showing tomorrow, Mrs. Outerbridge?"

"Gold-laced bantams," she said, as if Harriet ought to have known.

"I wish you the best of luck," Harriet replied.

"And you," Mrs. Outerbridge said—too distinctly. As if it were secretly a curse.

Harriet shook her head after the older woman went away. "The good folk of Bickerton are certainly known for their hospitality."

Lydia snorted and opened her mouth for what Harriet assumed would be a tart reply—but was interrupted by the arrival of a very short man in a very tall hat. "Miss Wraxhall! What's this I hear about you telling everyone you've found the lost Bickerton breed?" he demanded, his mustaches quivering with jollity.

"Good morning, Mr. Brome," Lydia said. She had on that too-bright smile again; Harriet was beginning to think of it as a weapon. The doctor's daughter waved her hand at her birds, a showman lifting the curtain. "The rumors are true."

"Silver-laced—going up against my champions, I see." He laughed, a shade too loudly, and his eyes were as sharp and bright as Lydia's smile. "You sly girl, just how long have you been keeping this secret for?"

"Hardly a secret, now that I'm here."

"Are there more?" He bent closer, his grin turning positively avaricious beneath the broom of his mustache. "Have you any chicks for sale? The Greys are notoriously true breeders, if memory serves."

"Mr. Brome, surely you're not asking me to set a price before the judging's even started?" Lydia had explained to Harriet how prize birds and eggs from the same were often sold off to help breed the next year's champions. A winning bird naturally brought in more money than one that failed to place.

Mr. Brome laughed again: "Ho ho, of course not! Wouldn't dream of trying to steal a march on you, Miss Wraxhall."

Harriet could all but hear Lydia's teeth grinding. "Glad to hear it, Mr. Brome."

And so it went, all the rest of the morning: Harriet was introduced to Mrs. Campbell-Cole, rival to Mr. Finglass (whom Harriet at least had met before), to the tall, stern Miss Inch (whom Harriet peered at very closely indeed, remembering that this was one of the women in Lydia's past), to Miss Rushcliff (a beauty who ignored Miss Inch with such vicious intensity that it was like a violin-string stretched humming between the two of them). Mrs. Outerbridge kept strolling by to glare at the Greys, and everyone was wielding polite phrases as though they were dueling swords and everyone's honor was being impugned.

By the time Mr. Finglass started arguing with the workmen about the best way to support the tent—the workmen wanted several towers of strength inside the structure, while Mr. Finglass thought they spoiled the aesthetics of the show and was demanding gye ropes and support poles on the tent's exterior—Harriet had had quite enough.

It felt, she realized, like the same fearful, brash hostility you got before a battle—the same eager, angry buzz in the air, the same thirst for blood and quickness to do harm. She could almost hear the cannons, smell the smoke again. Except Harriet kept looking around and: it was chickens. That's all. A lot of very pretty, very tasty birds. Not land, not politics, not any kind of a cause.

Harriet hated war, but she thought she might learn to hate this too, given time. She felt all those broken places in her heart creak, the surface of a frozen pond just about to give way and plunge her into deadly cold.

The worst part: Lydia seemed just as affected as everyone else. The sunny spirits Harriet had—oh, dear—that Harriet had fallen in love with were bubbling in the tent like acid in some chemist's laboratory. "Did your brother ever compete?"

Lydia's mouth softened at the mention of Peter. "He was in the army and across the world before the hen fever really took hold in the village—I kept him apprised of all my successes, though. Like the first year I entered, when I swept the cup for best collection out from under Mr. Finglass's nose. Or the year after that, when the top three Cochins were all my birds." She smirked, her satisfaction still potent after who knew how long. "Mrs. Outerbridge still holds a grudge about that one."

Harriet had met Mrs. Outerbridge, and did not care for Mrs. Outerbridge—but it made her uneasy to think of Lydia holding onto dislike with both hands for so many years. Lydia was supposed to be warm and welcoming; it was Harriet who was cold and standoffish.

Lydia waved cheerfully at Mrs. Outerbridge, whose narrowed eyes said she found the gesture suspicious. As she should: Lydia certainly didn't mean it.

"I told you the poultry fair was competitive," Lydia said, when Harriet ventured to say that perhaps Miss Rushcliff didn't mean anything nefarious by it when she said Minerva was a very lovely hen.

"This isn't competition," Harriet grumbled. "It's combat."

"So you should feel right at home," Lydia said with a laugh.

Harriet's head snapped back with the shock. Her hands went numb.

Lydia didn't notice; she was too busy eyeing the Pinwheel Bantams Miss Inch was brushing out two tables away.

Harriet felt a flash of sudden anger. "I thought you were better than this," she said.

It was a mistake, she knew it as soon as she heard the words come out. She knew it twice over when Lydia's cheeks flushed and her mouth went thin with hurt. "You sound like my parents." Harriet made a noise to object to this, but Lydia wasn't finished. "I know you have been everywhere and seen everything, Mrs. Boyne, but this is a quiet town. The Poultry Fair is the most important event in the village year. What you do here—how you place, what prizes you win—it *matters*. This competition is the only thing that keeps me from feeling utterly invisible." She rested a hand on Walter's cage, and the rooster made soft, soothing sounds at her. "If you find the Fair so unpalatable, then you needn't show in it."

Harriet rocked back as if she'd been slapped. "Very well," she said at length. "You have your Bickerton Greys, all six of them, and clearly you have no need of me. I wish you every prize." It came out sounding more bitter than she meant it to; Lydia's eyes flashed with pain, and Harriet had to turn away. "I think I'll take the cart back to the Hall," she said. *When will I see you again?* was right there on the tip of her tongue.

She let the question die unasked.

~ ~ ~ ~

Lydia simpered and smirked at her fellow competitors. She said nice things just to irritate Mrs. Outerbridge. She said more nice things to puzzle Miss Inch, and added an opinion or two to the argument Mr. Finglass was—still!—having with the workmen about the tent. She brushed Minerva and Walter until their plumes gleamed, even though she knew she'd only have to do it again tomorrow. She kept her hands moving and her smile fixed even though, inside, her heart ached and flowered like a bruise.

Peter would have been ashamed of her. *It's combat*, Harriet had said, but Lydia had heard, *It's a game*. They weren't at all the same. People died in war. Harriet had seen battle first-hand—and for Lydia to treat that as a reason she ought to be comfortable, instead of a deeply painful reminder of a tragedy that still haunted her…

Well. She'd be lucky if Harriet ever spoke to her again.

It had been thoughtlessness, born of anticipation and distraction, but that was no excuse. Behind her sunny façade Lydia's mind went in circles the entire day, trying to find some way of righting things while she prepared and then overprepared for tomorrow's judging. And then she turned her steps homeward, but she couldn't make herself pass through the gate and into the house.

She had no idea how to mend this. But she had to try.

She stopped by the Cock and Apple, bought a pie—an apology pie? A late supper? Who knew?—and began the walk to Thornycroft Hall.

The sky was low and the light was strange. Lydia was glad of it: she couldn't have handled velvet black or peaceful stars. The hunkered clouds suited her; she felt sympathy with the way they curled and twisted back on themselves.

She was no stranger to a lover's quarrel. Usually it meant the end of an affair, some terrible piece of punctuation that marked the turn away from bliss and into something more final. She hoped this one was different.

She hadn't even told Harriet she loved her.

The words had been there for weeks now, just waiting to be said. But Lydia had been afraid—what good was the love of a village spinster whose only achievements were poultry-related? What could she possibly offer? Harriet had a home and a fortune and friends who loved her, and who had seen her through much harder trials than Lydia had ever faced. They'd journeyed half the world with her, while Lydia had cowered in Bickerton, the narrow movements forming her mind and heart to match.

A snowflake tumbled out of the sky and onto Lydia's cheek. She let a tear fall and wash it away.

A hen in a coop, she was—falling in love with a lark.

She'd been so wrapped up in the strife, she hadn't been able to see the truth of what Harriet observed. Lydia had mistaken the rivalry for the real substance of the competition. After all, if her birds were good enough to win prizes, they'd win them without Lydia making sidelong remarks to Miss Rushcliff, or tormenting Mrs. Outerbridge, or needling Mr. Brome. None of that was necessary. None of it made anyone's life better.

Calling it a battle had been an excuse to justify a long habit of unkindness, and now Lydia was ashamed. Perhaps that had been part of the attraction all along: the Poultry Fair was the one time where nobody expected Lydia to be *nice*. Every other day of the year she held her tongue, did her duty, followed all the proper rules. Anger, self-interest, stubbornness—these she'd saved up to flourish like a rapier on Fair days.

Harriet had said it best: Lydia was better than that.

The Thornycroft Hall ballroom was dark, so Lydia went the long way around to the back of the house. Mrs. Crangle wasn't at all surprised to see her. "Boyne's in the parlor," she said, and eyed the pie with an expert's evaluatory gleam. "Is that for me?"

"Who else?" Lydia said, with the first real smile she'd enjoyed all day.

It didn't last long, though. She went out of the kitchen and into the front parlor, and there was Harriet, and still Lydia had no idea what she was going to say.

Harriet looked up from her book. Surprise, then relief, then regret chased across her face, swift as clouds scudding across a stormy sky.

And suddenly it was easy. "I came to apologize—" Lydia said.

"I am so sorry—" Harriet began, at precisely the same moment.

They broke off, flustered and awkward. But Harriet's eyes were glowing, and Lydia's heart felt feather-light. "You were right," she said. "And I am sorry."

"So am I," Harriet said, and held out her hands.

Lydia all but flew forward. Her arms went around Harriet's shoulders, and Harriet leaned forward to press her head to Lydia's breast. They stayed there a long while, breathing hard, as though they'd just fought their way free of the rapids of some flood-swollen river.

"I didn't hope to see you tonight," Harriet murmured.

"I couldn't bear not to come," Lydia replied. She combed Harriet's chestnut hair back from her temples, tilting her head back until their eyes met. "How could I rest knowing I'd hurt you?"

Harriet shook her head. "It was nothing."

"It was," Lydia insisted gently. She trailed her fingertips over Harriet's chin and cheeks. "I spent all day thinking about what you said—and seeing the truth of it. I ought to have listened better." She sighed. "I ought to have behaved better without you having to point it out to me."

Harriet shook her head, within the frame of Lydia's hands. "Your brother always said you were the best person he'd ever known. I see why, now."

Lydia snorted. "Are we talking about the same Lydia Wraxhall? The one who reveled in how bitter Mrs. Outerbridge has been about us resurrecting the lost Bickerton breed?"

"It's not wrong to take satisfaction in something wonderful," Harriet said. "What you're doing with the Greys is extraordinary. You deserve to be celebrated for that—not to be nitpicked, just because..." Her mouth flattened. "Just because sometimes the thought of any kind of fighting, even ordinary human disagreement, feels so exhausting I could sink down to the earth and never move again. That's not your fault: it's mine." She glanced up, her grey eyes glinting. "Mrs. Outerbridge is just the kind of petty tyrant who grinds down the spirits of everyone around her—she's worth pushing back against, if only to show other people that it can be done."

"Oh yes, make a virtue out of my worst habit," Lydia said, with a laugh. "No wonder I adore you."

Harriet froze.

Lydia waited, breath held.

A soft sound from behind them, as someone cleared a throat. "Pardon the interruption," Mrs. Crangle said, voice bone-dry. "I suppose I'll be sitting up with Arun tonight?"

"Tonight?" Harriet said, peering around Lydia. "Why?"

"Haven't you looked outside?"

Harriet went to the window and pulled back the curtain.

Outside: a blizzard.

Lydia gasped. "Walter," she said. "The tent!"

She sprinted into the hall and yanked open the front door.

Wind and snow swirled around, sending her skirts whipping about her legs. The cold tore at her throat and bit at her hands. Lydia sucked in a breath and the winter burned her lungs, plucked at the hair pinned up on her head.

And a mile away were seven chickens of hers—and everyone else's, four whole rows of carefully bred creatures—with only a tent between them and this fierce clash of elements.

Lydia made it one step over the threshold before a hand grasped her arm and dragged her back. "Are you mad?" Harriet cried. "You can't go out in that!"

Lydia shook her head. "Someone has to try and—"

"For God's sake, woman, are you not more important than chickens?" Harriet's voice dropped into a low rasp. "Even to yourself?"

Lydia stilled, breathing raggedly.

Harriet's hand held her arm, and now the other cupped Lydia's cheek. "There are people in the village, closer to the tent, who can help," she said. "If you try and make it to Bickerton through this weather, you'll be lost before you reach the road."

Lydia shook her head, because she knew it was true. She just wished it weren't.

Harriet's voice was low, but clear as a bell: "Listen to someone who loves you," she said. "Stay."

Lydia made a wild, wordless sound, turned, and flung herself against Harriet's chest.

Mrs. Crangle snorted and strode around the pair of them to pull the front door shut. Snowflakes settled gently to the stone, and the hush from the lack of wind was deafening. "If you've got all that sorted out," she said, making Harriet grin and Lydia blush, "I'll be going up." Then the older woman did just that, climbing the broad stairs with one last indulgent shake of her head.

Lydia and Harriet stayed in the hall a little longer. The biting cold from the wind still lingered in Lydia's hair, and she could feel an echo of it on Harriet's skin when she nuzzled into Harriet's throat. She pressed her mouth there to heat it away. "You love me," she said, wonderingly.

"You sound surprised."

"Pleased, more like."

Harriet's voice went low and honey-sweet. "How pleased?"

Lydia grinned and scraped her teeth across the tender skin of her beloved's throat. Harriet laughed a breathy sound, like the wind in branches—and pulled her up the stairs to bed.

Much later, Lydia asked: "Why is Mrs. Crangle staying up with Mr. Dixit?"

"He has trouble with storms," Harriet said. They were sprawled over one another across the bed, coverlet askew, limbs flung every which way. "He was on a ship in Balaklava harbor last winter when a hurricane came through. The destruction was… unimaginable. He was lucky to have survived—and ever since, he cannot abide storms or confined spaces."

Lydia held her tighter. "He's lucky to have friends who understand what he's gone through."

"It's not only him," Harriet said. Her hands were moving, restless over Lydia's skin. "We're all carrying the war around with us, still, in different ways. I'm not sure the breaks will ever heal completely."

"You aren't broken," Lydia insisted, and then again when Harriet shook her head. "You aren't. You're—changed, that's all. The world changes you, changes all of us." She wrapped her arms around Harriet's waist, head resting on the hollow of her collarbone, perfectly sculpted for Lydia's cheek. "When we lost Peter, I knew things would never be the same. Not for my parents or myself. It's always going to be a part of us now, that grief. That hurt."

"Grief can be the sharpest weapon of all," Harriet murmured.

"Grief is not something that exists outside of people," Lydia countered. "That's what I'm trying to say—the grief is not a thing that happens to you. It is a part of you. Us."

Harriet huffed, amusement and chagrin mingled in her voice. "You're saying we do this to ourselves."

"I'm saying: you can't grieve where you haven't loved." She raised her head. "You're worried the war is part of you."

Harriet's head jerked once, affirming. She looked away, chin high.

Lydia smiled fondly. "You don't have to love the war. But you can—you must—love the part of you that carries it."

Harriet's eyes were wide.

Lydia lowered her head again, listening to the wind howl against the windowpanes. "I've never seen a battlefield," she said. "But I've sat at plenty of deathbeds. There are ghosts I carry around with me—people nobody else remembers, but who I see whenever I turn a corner in the road, or walk past a house in the village. You could fill Bickerton twice over with just the people whose last words I was the only one there to listen to." Harriet's hand tightened on Lydia's shoulder, offering comfort. "If I tried to shut those memories away, I'd lose half of myself. I expect it's the same for you, and for the others in this house." She scooted up, resting one elbow beneath her, and fixing Harriet with a gaze that left no room for doubt or fear. "You carry the war with you," Lydia said, "because you were strong enough to survive it."

Harriet breathed out. "Lucky. Not strong."

Lydia shrugged. "Lucky *and* strong, then."

"Lucky," Harriet repeated, and her hands threaded in Lydia's hair, and her eyes shone, and her smile was a bonfire and a seduction and a sun. "Lucky enough to find you."

he storm lasted through the night and most of the morning, then pulled away like a curtain to let the winter sunlight flood the snow-muffled hills. Lydia had been up since dawn, so Harriet fed her lunch and wrapped her in her thickest cloak and followed her out into the wide, white world.

Half a foot of snow had changed the contours of the hills; they were taller but somehow softer, velvet heaps to either side of the road. Harriet was exhausted by the time they reached Bickerton green, where they found a fretting, fluttering crowd of poultry enthusiasts picking through the ruins of the tent.

Harriet's heart stuttered; Lydia gave a cry and ran forward.

Mr. Finglass was where she'd left him, at the front where the tent had collapsed like a wave breaking on the shore, arguing with the head workman—Harriet had an improbable, unshakeable vision the two of them had been fixed there all night, arguing, as the storm raged and roared around them. "I told you," the weary workman was saying, "we needed more towers of strength—"

Lydia went to where Mr. Brome was standing beside a mass of tumbled tables and wrecked cages, the willow-work bent and twisted. A handful of small feathered bodies had been carefully laid to one side, but not nearly as many as Harriet thought there ought to have been. "How bad is it?" Lydia was asking as Harriet caught up.

"I can't figure it," Mr. Brome said, mustache trembling beneath a lugubrious eye. "They seem to have vanished."

"What," Lydia said, "all of them?"

"Most," he confirmed. "I don't think we've found half a dozen birds all together. Though I suppose the snow could be covering some—but still, that's a lot of birds left to look for."

Harriet picked up one stray feather. Silver lacing, in a familiar pattern. She looked around—and there, another one, toward the side of the tent nearest the church.

And there, through the tiny ancient graveyard—a track. The kind a flock of marching birds might make, as they struggled through snow.

"Lydia," she breathed. "Look!"

Lydia did look, blinking, and hope burst warm onto her face. "You think… the abbey?" she asked.

"Worth checking, I'd say."

"You're free to chase those wild hens all the way to Dover, if you want," Mr. Brome said, when they asked if he might like to join them in search of his lost bantams. "Mine are more likely to be found somewhere closer to home. They're civilized birds," he said, sniffing.

"I'll be heading into the wood," Miss Inch said with a huff. "Mine have a tendency to try to run that way."

Miss Rushcliff's brow furrowed and she bit her lip, but said nothing.

All the competitors broke apart, with many a glance of mutual suspicion and wariness.

The search was underway.

Mr. Brome went directly home, on the assumption his respectable chickens would do the same. And indeed, his yard was full of birds, who had climbed in thanks to a snowbank the wind had piled high against one of the fences. But instead of cool grey plumage, these were laced bright gold.

He harrumphed into his mustache. These weren't his birds at all.

The interlopers were milling about, still looking a little wild about the eye, and scratching at the snow where the dirt of the yard showed through. Mr. Brome tsked and fetched a bit of feed, scattering dried corn and grains and a lump of fat that the birds immediately dove for.

"Oh," said a voice behind him.

Mr. Brome spun about to see—who else?—Matilda Outerbridge standing there, one hand on his gate. Surprise softened her features, made her parted lips lush rather than the thin line he was more used to.

He didn't like that she looked so—human. "I'll thank you to remove your birds from my yard, Mrs. Outerbridge."

She drew herself up, and he felt an unaccountable relief to see her armor slot back into place. It made him uneasy when she was vulnerable. It was too like tenderness—and tenderness meant hurt, and hurt reminded him of the old days, when every breath had felt painful—

No. Better to be safe, even if it was a little lonely at times.

But then it was his turn to be surprised.

"Thank you for feeding them, Mr. Brome," she said.

He blinked. That had sounded—sincere. A bit snobbish, perhaps, the way a queen would thank a subject for obeisance, but it lacked her usual venom. He tried to bring back a little of his own. "I hope you don't think I'd punish an innocent chicken for the sins of her mistress."

"I would have expected precisely that, sir." That hard, thin line was back on her mouth. It was less reassuring this time, for some reason. The chill of every winter was in her voice when she went on: "You've been doing just that for the past ten years."

Mr. Brome bristled, stung in a way that never seemed to get any easier, no matter how much time passed. "I wish they'd never crossed over my threshold, Mrs. Outerbridge, and that's the truth."

She looked at him a long while. "Are we still talking about the chickens?"

"The chickens, and."

"The chickens, and," she repeated, and her stern mouth wobbled as she sucked in a deep breath.

Mr. Brome looked away. "Your birds might as well stay here for now," he said. "Since my own are still out there somewhere."

Mrs. Outerbridge's shoulders straightened. Mr. Brome had always thought she'd have made a fine and frightening general, were she not a woman, and nothing in her posture now dissuaded him of the idea. "Then let us find your birds, Mr. Brome."

"You're offering to help?"

She sniffed, but the sound didn't set his teeth on edge like it had before. Odd, that. "I am offering to accompany you in the search, so that you will not put my birds out into the snow as soon as your own are back in the coop where they belong." She peered at the far side of the yard, where the fence was high and undamaged. "Where do you suppose they'll have gone to?"

Mr. Brome chewed his mustache in irritation. "That Wraxhall girl was saying something about the abbey."

"That's a good half mile away," Mrs. Outerbridge said, and spun on her heel. "We'd best get started."

Mr. Brome, like any good soldier, fell in line.

~ ~ ~ ~

Deep in the woods, Miss Inch was on the hunt. Her Pinwheel Bantams' plumage was bright and distinctive, and she'd caught sight of one of her cockerels not too far from the collapsed tent. It was either Reginald or Rothgar, she couldn't tell which without the other standing next to him. Whatever his name, he'd led her a merry chase into the wood, but now she was certain she had him cornered in a small dale at the base of the hill. Trapped between the sharp shadows of the holly bushes on the one side, and on the other a fallen log overgrown with mushrooms and moss.

Miss Inch slowly set her lantern down, flexed her hands in her woolen mittens, and seized the chicken.

At least, that was the intention.

At precisely the moment she moved, the cockerel dove sideways, crying out in alarm and kicking up a dust of snow and needle-edged leaves with the force of his flapping wings. Miss Inch tried to alter course mid-gesture, following the bird's movement—he just brushed the tips of her outstretched mittens as he slipped around her and dove for escape back down the path she'd followed.

Miss Inch caught sight of a flash of vivid red, just before her bad knee gave out and she flopped face-first into a snowbank with what she feared was an abysmal lack of grace, elegance, or basic dignity.

Another squawk from the cockerel—damn him—and then an even more unwelcome sound. "Is that you, Miss Inch?"

She knew that voice at once.

For a moment, Miss Inch thought she just might lie there on the ground until the snow melted and she could slink home and lock herself in her room and succumb to a fatal bout of embarrassment. That voice had once laughed at her jokes, even the bad ones. That voice had once whispered naughty things across the soft, lace-edged lawn of a pillowcase, and loving words beneath the boughs of a tree in spring. But its vowels were cold as winter now, its consonants sharp as ice.

Miss Inch's nose had gone numb, which was a bad sign, and her breath had melted enough of the snow to trickle beneath the wool of her scarf and ice the soft skin of her throat. She jerked herself upright on instinct, then wished she hadn't.

Miss Rushcliff was standing there, her coat blood-red and aggressive against the white and black and evergreens, and she held Reginald-or-Rothgar prisoner, his crown of plumage a starburst or a dahlia or a rose in dark-gloved hands that Miss Inch once had loved. Her eyes were wide beneath the curve of her bonnet and the black velvet ribbon tied beneath her chin. "Are you all right?" she asked.

Miss Rushcliff—*Caro*, whispered some traitorous memory—had been pretty at age twenty, but now at five-and-thirty she had matured into the richness of true beauty. The way wine became brandy, with time. And heat.

Miss Inch squelched the memories of heat, pushed herself up, and tried to brush the snow from the wool of her coat. It clung, frustrating her, and with a huff she gave up the attempt. Her bad knee was a throb of pain; she put all her weight on her other leg and tried to ignore it. "Thank you for catching my cockerel," Miss Inch said. "If you'll hand him over, I needn't keep you from your own search."

Miss Rushcliff blinked, and appeared to shake off some spell. "Of course," she said, and held out the bird.

Miss Inch reached out, glad the thick wool of her mittens hid how her own hands were shaking. She shuffled a step sideways, trying to grasp the body of her bird without putting her hands over Miss Rushcliff's.

She couldn't bear the thought of touching her again and having the shaking of her hands betray what she was really feeling. Even through two layers of wool and leather, she feared Miss Rushcliff would know.

She'd always been able to see through Miss Inch's bravado. Once, that had been a pleasure, a secret game the two of them could play even when there were others about.

Now, it was a knife to a heart that refused to stop beating no matter how many times it was pierced.

Miss Inch had gotten her angles wrong, however. Reginald-or-Rothgar saw his chance and took it. With a wrench and a toss of his plumed head, he twisted free of both women's grasp and pelted between two birch trees and up the hill to the east.

And he had vengeance, as well as escape: that twisting trick of his had left Miss Inch's and Miss Rushcliff's hands entangled.

Too close, after too long, and the silence of the woods felt like the old kind of secrecy. Miss Rushcliff's gasp was soft, but it might as well have been a peal of thunder for the way it shook Miss Inch down to her bones.

She yanked her hands back. "I'm so sorry!" Ugh, she was hopeless. What was she even apologizing for?

Miss Rushcliff's gloved hands opened and closed, then fell back to her side. "I should be the one apologizing," she said. A faint crease appeared between her eyes. "Are you sure you're all right?"

"Quite sure," Miss Inch said—then spoiled it by wobbling as her bad knee gave out and she had to catch herself before she fell. Again.

Where was an earthquake to swallow a girl when she needed it?

A hand caught her elbow, steadying her. Even the wind in the trees seemed to hold its breath.

Miss Inch looked up into Miss Rushcliff's blue eyes, so full of concern. And something else: regret? Shame? That couldn't be right. "Your knee again?" she asked knowingly.

"Been a little worse this winter," Miss Inch muttered, cheeks flushed.

Miss Rushcliff's lovely mouth firmed in that stubborn way that Miss Inch had always—even now—admired beyond the bounds of reason. "I'm not leaving you out here alone when you can't walk," she said, and apparently that was that. She linked her arm beneath Miss Inch's, and just like that the world was steady again. And warm, with someone's body there to keep the wind from reaching her side. "Now," Miss Rushcliff said, "did you see which way your cockerel went?"

~ ~ ~ ~

"Unbelievable," Harriet muttered.

Lydia could only laugh, muffling it behind her hand to keep from spooking the birds.

Unlike the others, Harriet and Lydia had gone directly to the abbey. So they were the first to find, huddled up against the stone walls, all of Bickerton's lost chickens.

Gold-laced, silver-laced, Brahmas and bantams and Scots Dumpies, every variety had been herded up the hill and into the ruins. Lydia's Bickerton Grey hens were patrolling the line, keeping all the other chickens within the walls by a ruthless use of pecks and clucks and scratches.

Walter was standing on a stone a little raised, looking over the enormous flock with a dim but distinctly paternal eye.

"Chickens are creatures of habit," Lydia murmured, amusement warming her voice like brandy in coffee.

"Our hens appear to be creatures of command," Harriet returned, shielding her eyes from the glare of sun on snow and trying to count chickens.

Soon other searchers appeared out of the wood and from the hills, as other chicken fanciers followed the trails that all converged on the abbey stones.

Mrs. Outerbridge was first to arrive, storming up the snow-decked slope like an icebreaker with Mr. Brome ambling in her wake. Miss Rushcliff helped a limping Miss Inch step by slow step —it seemed they were taking a little longer and staying a little closer than was strictly necessary—and then Mr. Finglass, Mr. and Mrs. Campbell-Cole, Mr. Kaur and his sister, and all the other Bickerton chicken fanciers that Harriet hadn't had a chance to meet yet.

Breath steaming, they clumped together in the aisle of what had once been a church, and contemplated the milling, clucking, occasionally growling horde of birds. Walter bokked in warning as Mr. Brome took a step forward, and settled when Mr. Brome took a step back.

It was one of those rare moments where everyone there was thinking the same thing and knew it: as soon as they tried to grab one chicken, any chicken, Walter would sound the alarm cry, and absolute chaos would erupt.

"Well," said Mrs. Outerbridge eventually, "we have to do something."

"Do we?" Mr. Brome muttered. "I do not like the look in that rooster's eye."

"He's harmless," Lydia said.

Mr. Brome glowered. "To you, perhaps."

"We can't just leave them here," Miss Rushcliff sighed.

"They look pretty cozy," Miss Inch countered, pointing at a pile where a Pinwheel Bantam was draped in all its feathered glory over the short, squat bulk of a Scots Dumpie. Miss Rushcliff giggled.

Lydia shivered as a particularly chill wind passed over the stones.

The snow, the wind, and the ruins brought Harriet back to a bad moment from the war. For a moment her throat closed and she couldn't catch her breath—but then Lydia tucked close against her side, and that little bit of heat seeped into Harriet's heart and nestled there. The way she'd learned a hen returned to its home coop.

Even if that coop was a falling-down abbey in the middle of a snowstorm.

She shook her head. "How on earth are we going to get so many birds back to their proper homes?"

Lydia grinned. "Wait until nightfall?"

Harriet groaned. "You had me the first time, but I'm not falling for that nonsense again."

"What nonsense?" Mrs. Outerbridge demanded.

Harriet flushed. "She had my friends and I out here in the dark with lanterns, hoping to catch chickens."

But to her shock, Mrs. Outerbridge only nodded. "Eminently sensible," she said. "Miss Wraxhall always did have a good head on her shoulders."

"Best way," Mr. Brome agreed. "Tired birds are more easily managed."

"But that's hours away," Miss Inch said, wincing as she inadvertently leaned on her injured leg.

Harriet caught Lydia's eye. It was twinkling, starlike, and her beloved's expression was so full of unspoken hope and pleading that it made Harriet want to laugh or cry, she wasn't sure which. Harriet was helpless before that unasked question.

"Fine," she said for Lydia's ears alone—then raised her voice and pitched it to carry over the entirety of the crowd. "Ladies and gentlemen and chicken fanciers all—may I invite you to Christmas Eve dinner while we wait until nightfall?"

Mr. Finglass and Mr. Kaur took the first watch, so the chickens would not be left alone to wander further. Everyone else followed Harriet and Lydia down one hill and around another to the door of Thornycroft Hall. Lydia led them into the ballroom—the only room big enough for such a crowd—while Harriet went to find Lizzie Crangle and see what they could do for a dinner.

Mrs. Crangle was ecstatic, and did not disappoint. She sent up a dozen cold meat and pigeon pies at once, then rolled her sleeves to the elbow and raided the larder and got the undercooks scampering. Harriet went to the cellar to select wine and brandy and punch, and between that and the pies the chicken fanciers were having a grand feast even before Mrs. Crangle began laying out dishes on the long table the footmen Sam and Stephen had hastily erected on the short side of the ballroom. Mr. Dixit and Mrs. Goodfellow joined the party, eyes wide and delighted at the sudden influx of visitors. Mrs. Marwood even poked her head in, drawn by the sounds of merriment; she stole the last pigeon pie before Harriet could claim it and vanished back upstairs before Harriet had even stopped laughing.

Mrs. Outerbridge pulled the dust cloth from the piano and

began playing carols with a surprising amount of verve, while Miss Inch turned the pages and Miss Rushcliff sang a rather good alto.

It was loud and busy and warm and the best time Harriet had ever had.

Everywhere she looked, the same rivals who'd been glaring daggers at one another this morning were arm in arm singing harmony, or laughing at someone's story, or dancing an impromptu waltz to Mrs. Outerbridge's accompaniment.

And maybe this was a temporary truce only, and wouldn't last —but she hoped not. She wanted this to be the start of something better for the whole village. They all deserved that much, and more.

Eventually Mr. Brome and Mr. Campbell-Cole went to relieve Mr. Kaur and Mr. Finglass—the pair returned escorting the baffled Birmingham judges, whose train had been delayed by the storm. But they were happy enough to leave chicken points for another day and take part in the general merriment. One judge, a Mr. Upperton, whose eye was apparently very fierce on the finer points of a Brahma bird, had so much brandy and roast goose that he tried to award the great silver cup to Harriet as a champion hostess.

"Just wait until next year," Lydia said, as Harriet laughingly declined the honor. "You'll win that cup in earnest, I'll make sure of it."

Harriet squeezed her hand, face aching from too much smiling. "Oh will you?"

"Of course—after all, we've got a whole breed of birds to revive. That's going to take some doing!" She grinned, eyes sparkling at the thought of what the future held. "We're going to have so many chicks this spring. We might have to expand the chicken run a bit."

Harriet smiled slyly. "Would you say there's enough work that it would make sense for you to move in here, with us?" Lydia froze. Harriet pressed onward. "After all, we'll need someone with experience to oversee any expansion of the yard, and none of us know anything about crossbreeding. It's sure to save time if you don't have to walk back and forth every day." She lowered her voice. "And there are other benefits, of course…"

"Do you mean it?" Lydia asked. Her voice was quiet, but Harriet could her her hope and fear so clearly despite all the background cacophony. "You wouldn't mind?"

Harriet laughed and hugged her close. There, in the circle of her arms, where only the two of them could hear, she whispered, "My love, I would be delighted."

Lydia trembled, and Harriet wanted nothing more than to kiss her silly—but that would have to wait until later.

Eventually nightfall came, and the feast came to an end. Harriet brought out Thornycroft Hall's supply of lanterns— ancient and a little rusted in places, but still useful—and as many carts and wheelbarrows and wagons as the Hall could supply. They repurposed wooden feed crates into makeshift chicken cages for the journey home, and soon everyone was trekking back to the abbey, whispering and giggling softly and trying to be quiet as they crunched over the snow. Lanterns bobbed across the landscape as the fanciers spread out, until the hill was covered with points of light like a mirror of the stars above. The chickens were a sleeping, snoring pile by this time, and one by one the fanciers carefully seized their sleeping birds. Farewells were whispered, and good-nights, and after an hour it was only Lydia and Harriet and their seven chickens, crated in the last wheelbarrow, trundling back to the Hall.

Harriet was pushing the wheelbarrow; Lydia was looking up at the night sky. "I think this was the best poultry fair yet," she said.

Harriet smiled, and her heart burned like the sun. "Wait until next year."

ABOUT THE AUTHOR

Olivia Waite writes queer historical romance, fantasy, science fiction, and essays. She is the romance fiction columnist for the New York Times Book Review.

When the birds are propitious, she sends out the <u>Oliviary</u>: a newsletter with timely updates, recommended reads, and intriguing content curated from niche corners of the internet.

ALSO BY OLIVIA WAITE

Generous Fire

The Best Worst Holiday Party Ever

The Feminine Pursuits Series:
The Lady's Guide to Celestial Mechanics
The Care and Feeding of Waspish Widows
The Hellion's Waltz

A Thief in the Nude and
At His Countess's Pleasure

Happily Ever Afterlives

Hearts and Harbingers

www.ingramcontent.com/pod-product-compliance
Lightning Source LLC
Chambersburg PA
CBHW070643130626

46555CB00006B/2675